Peter is a young man who loves art and writing, and has successfully combined these skills in his first self-illustrated novel for children.

He has faced significant challenges due to his diagnosis of Autism and Tourette Syndrome, but with support and encouragement is truly beginning to flourish and find his voice.

Peter has a long-held ambition to write and narrate stories for children to make them happy, and to be an illustrator. This first Pooky novel is the start of realizing that dream.

This is dedicated to Peter's Uncle George, who died suddenly and unexpectedly during the time he was writing the novel.

Peter Spencer

POOKY BEAUMONT AND THE WIZARD'S DASTARDLY PLOT

AUSTIN MACAULEY PUBLISHERS™

LONDON * CAMBRIDGE * NEW YORK * SHARJAH

A CIP catalogue record for this title is available from the British Library.

ISBN 9781398441354 (Paperback)
ISBN 9781398441361 (Hardback)
ISBN 9781398441385 (ePub e-book)
ISBN 9781398441378 (Audiobook)

www.austinmacauley.com

First Published 2023
Austin Macauley Publishers Ltd®
1 Canada Square
Canary Wharf
London
E14 5AA

Peter would like to thank his family for their support and encouragement, and to Jaris Ash of Pag-e-nation who worked with him and started him on his journey of realizing his dream of becoming a published author and illustrator.

Table of Contents

Chapter 1: Pooky's Life   11

Chapter 2: The Beaumont Family   14

Chapter 3: The Poo Factory   18

Chapter 4: The School Bullies   21

Chapter 5: The Horrible Prank   24

Chapter 6: Miss Hurricane – The Headmistress   30

Chapter 7: The Shock   32

Chapter 8: Cleaning Pooky   34

Chapter 9: Amrita Comes To Dinner   37

Chapter 10: Pooky In Trouble   41

Chapter 11: The Stern Talk   46

Chapter 12: The Midnight Talk   48

Chapter 13: Looking After Pooky   52

Chapter 14: A Visit From The Doctor   55

Chapter 15: Spending Time With Pooky   58

Chapter 16: Pooky And Percy   60

Chapter 17: Sharing Stories   64

Chapter 18: The Discovery   68

Chapter 19: Setting The Trap   72

Chapter 20: The New Slave   76

Chapter 21: The Crime Scene   79

Chapter 22: The Very Sad News   82

Chapter 23: Pooky's Terrible Work   85

Chapter 24: Pooky Cleans Up   89

Chapter 25: Pooky's Wish   **91**

Chapter 26: The Secret Is Now Revealed   **93**

Chapter 27: The Meeting   **97**

Chapter 28: The Confused Wizard   **100**

Chapter 29: The Magical Battle   **104**

Chapter 30: The Colourful Explosion   **107**

Chapter 31: A Happy Reunion   **113**

Chapter 32: Pooky's Welcome Home Party   **115**

Chapter 33: A Happy Event   **119**

Pookistory   **125**

Chapter 1
Pooky's Life

Once upon a time, in merry old Victorian England of 1888, there lived a beautiful little eight-year-old girl called Pooky Beaumont. She was a very good and well-behaved girl and she lived in a magnificent house in Holland Park Avenue with

her wonderful family. Pooky was very good at hobbies and loved helping both around the house and her friends and neighbours in the street. Now, you may wonder why she was called Pooky.

Well, the reason is that, hmm, how can I put this, because it had the word poo in her name. Yes! Unfortunately, it was a real problem for her. Also some of the children thought that it was very funny to have a girl with that name. There are other pretty names for girls, like flowers and months or being named after a person. Then you can call her Phoebe or Poppy or Primrose or any other girl's names that you can think of. But it's not that easy to name a girl who is special, so that is why we call her Pooky.

She had two big brothers and their names were Donald and Douglas. They're twins, of course. They had a wonderful mother called Penelope and a great father called Jack. The house that they lived in was a mansion; they had a kind butler called Igor and two pretty housemaids whose names were Mitzi and Sophie. They even had a terrific cook named Remy, and he was a genius at making excellent meals for the family and guests. I'll explain about them in a couple of minutes.

Now, Pooky's life at home was quite lovely and perfect, but the real problem was that she was bullied at her school, which I will also tell you about.

Sometimes, Pooky was very sad and felt as if she didn't fit in with the children at school. What I am trying to say is that they were making Pooky's life a misery and none of them wanted to be friends with her.

All except for a girl called Amrita who was a good friend to Pooky. Amrita was a nice nine-year old girl. She and her family had moved from India after her old home was destroyed, and now they lived and worked happily in London. Amrita didn't like anyone bullying Pooky and she felt sorry for her.

So, you see, Pooky did have a friend to talk to, but that's not the main problem, as I've explained to you before. Not only was she being bullied, but two horrid boys kept teasing her as well as being nasty and rude, and this is where the story about Pooky begins.

Chapter 2
The Beaumont Family

Pooky's family was very rich, and they always tried to help the poor people around Holland Park Avenue.

Pooky's mother, Penelope Beaumont, was a councillor's assistant and always sorted out the paperwork and meetings for people who came to talk to the councillor.

She was very quick at completing her job and never got it wrong. She even spent time with her family at the end of every day, especially Pooky.

Donald and Douglas, Pooky's big brothers, went to the same school as their beautiful little sister.

Their father, Jack Beaumont, worked as an engine driver on the Great Western Railway, taking and helping the passengers, shunting lots of trucks and delivering goods to all of his neighbours and friends around the centre of London and lots of other places. Igor, the Beaumonts' butler, was a kind and handsome man. He opened the door and greeted lots of visitors and friends that came around for tea and chats with Jack and Penelope.

He gave messages to anybody in the house,

and, in his spare time, he sat in his chair in his study and read the Daily Telegraph Newspaper. Igor even helped the Beaumont children with their school homework and also gave them some kind advice on doing the right thing.

He had Tourettes, which made him a bit excited at times.

Everyone in the house understood this and they didn't mind at all, which made Igor feel better.

Remy was the Beaumonts cook. He was good at cooking lots of good, delicious food and liked to make everyone in the house very happy. His favourite was making Victoria cupcakes and he gave them to any visitors when they came to see the family.

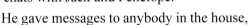

Mitzi and Sophie, the two housemaids, were very good maids. They cleaned the whole house from top to bottom, they served food and drinks to their masters and their guests. They washed, cleaned, and ironed their clothes and also helped the children get ready for school in the weekdays and ready for bed at night-time.

They also even disposed of their waste when they needed the bathroom, day, or night, especially Pooky's.

Everything was absolutely perfect, and they never had any problems at all.

Except for one, and that was poor Pooky.

Her parents and her brothers felt very worried and sorry for her. They knew that she was being bullied by the children at the Victorian School, and the two horrid boys, who I told you about earlier, were called Hector and Rocky. They were very horrid and rude little boys and they always made fun of Pooky, and they never left her alone.

Now, here's the problem. You see, Pooky always ate good food, and she always ate healthily, but sometimes after she had eaten, she got a little fart coming out of her bottom. It always happened when she was busy doing her school studies, chatting with the family, or going on any adventures. Luckily, she always managed to get to the toilet in time, upstairs or downstairs, and sat down on the toilet and relaxed until she felt better.

Pooky even had a chamber pot by her bed, so she could sit down on it when she was in her bedroom in the day or sometimes, she got up in the middle of the night. She even went to the toilet at school if she accidently farted quietly in lessons, but she always told her teacher before rushing off to the toilet.

Even her teacher and the Headmistress felt sorry for her.

But whenever Pooky felt a quiet fart, her family and friends were always there to help her.

Chapter 3
The Poo Factory

Over on the other side of London, there was a very old factory. It used to make clothes and blankets, but it had been empty for many years, and no one never went in or came out. Or did they?

This may be surprising to you, but up until now, the factory had been put to strange use by two weird people. These two people were very old and horrid. One of them was an evil wizard and the other an ugly old witch. They had lived and worked in the old factory for many years and made disgusting food.

Do you want to know why?

Well, they made the horrible food out of human poo with their magic ball, and they mixed it in their magic cauldron. The cauldron was big and huge as the size of a fountain. They even kept some of the food for themselves.

Now, let me explain how all the human poo ended up at the old factory. You may have heard of the night soil men. They shovelled the poo from the toilets onto their carts, and carried it out of any towns or cities, but the villains never did that. They magically disguised themselves as night soil people and travelled around London collecting the poo from people's houses and took it back to the factory. They worked all night, and then they began to make the disgusting food out of it. They had a very incredible machine for making lots and lots of horrible food.

So, how did it work, I hear you ask. Well, first they emptied the cart of poo down the shoot and then they threw some old and rotten food down as well.

When all of that was all put into the machine, they used their magic spells to make the food bigger and worse.

The wizard and the witch had a talking parrot called Percy. Percy was a very nice talking parrot, but he absolutely hated working with the villains and he also hated the horrible smell of poo.

He even had to fly around the factory carrying a heavy bucket from the toilets to the machine.

If he didn't do as he was told, they would soon threaten him by telling him they would pull out his feathers and cut his wings and tail off. Percy didn't really like this, but he knew that he had no choice.

Sometimes, when the wizard and the witch ordered Percy to go outside for a while, he would happily stretch his wings and fly around the factory and take a deep breath with relief.

"Huh, that's better!" He smiled, as he perched himself on the roof of the poo factory. "That horrible smell is really making me sick!" Percy sighed and looked across the river at the City of London.

"I wish I could escape from this horrible, disgusting place and find a nice friendly family to live with," he sobbed sadly.

He dried his tears, flapped his wings, and flew back into the factory. As he perched on top of his cage, he saw the wizard talking to the witch in a quiet corner.

"We are not making progress," said the wizard grumpily, as he looked into the cauldron.

"Indeed!" replied the witch, as she made a clicking noise with her teeth. "What we need is someone to sit on the toilet in the prison cell who will keep on pooing and pooing until we have enough to make even more revolting food," she added thoughtfully.

"Hmmm, yes, that's a brilliant idea!" The wizard grinned. "But who would do it? Besides, we need a slave to do the dirty work." The witch sighed and thought again.

"Then we'll just have look around London until we've found the person to be our slave," she said. And with that, they left the room and went to the kitchen to eat. Percy, who was still on top of his cage, was worried and puzzled.

"What do they mean?" Percy wondered. "Who would be their slave in doing their dirty work?"

He decided that the best thing to do was to fly around London and keep an eye on the two nasty people as they went out to collect the poo from outside people's houses.

Chapter 4
The School Bullies

Now I will explain about the two horrid boys, Hector and Rocky, as I promised you earlier. Hector was a twelve-year-old boy. He was really a big show off, and he loved bullying, teasing, and picking on any child he could. His ginger hair was very scruffy and little bits of mud got stuck in it, but he usually rubbed and scratched his head to make his hair springy and fuzzy. Worst of all, he never washed his hair, except maybe on weekends. He even had a nasty habit. You see, when he ate and gobbled his food down, bits of food would fly everywhere in different directions, and some even landed in his hair.

Hector didn't bother to clean his mouth after he ate, which was a revolting result, and bits of old meal-time foods were glued to his hair. They were only small bits in fact, and sometimes, he used to clean them off with his hand or his handkerchief.

Now, if you look closely, remember to hold your nose just in case, because you would see objects that had been there for weeks or even months. Like a piece of mouldy old ham, or a rotten bit of bread, or a little strip of a chicken's skin.

After all, when Hector felt his tummy rumbling, he could scratch around his head and find a bit of old and rotten food to eat as a snack. That was really disgusting.

What I am trying to say is that Hector was a greedy and stubborn boy. He was also a very naughty boy, as was his best friend, Rocky.

Rocky was a ten-year old boy. He was even naughtier than Hector, and he was full of nasty horrid ideas for playing tricks and pranks on anybody and everybody he saw. No one was ever such a horrid little boy with mischievous tricks.

Before Rocky had an ugly face, he once had a nice face, but that was when he was a baby. He got uglier day after day, month after month and year after year. How on earth did it happen? Well, I'll explain it to you.

You see, if you have good thoughts, it will make your face very handsome and if anyone has some bad thoughts, it makes the face go ugly, and when it goes really ugly you can hardly not take any notice of it.

Rocky had nice teeth when he was four years old, but now he had got buckled and stuck-out teeth and his left eye had shrunk to the size of a plastic bead. He looked like a scary old monster and his hands were raw and had little purple spots because he'd been rubbing and scratching them when he had an itch. So, you see, Hector and Rocky were very, very, very naughty, and they always upset any child that they could pick on. But there was only one person that the horrid boys really loved to bully, and that was…yes…you're right, Pooky Beaumont.

Hector and Rocky loved bullying, teasing, and picking on poor old Pooky, and they kept calling her Poo because of the three letters in her name.

They even had drawings of rude pictures of Pooky on the toilet. They danced rudely around her, and worst of all, they even made-up rude songs about her. The song they sang sounded something like this:

"Pooky is a smelly girl,
Cause she has caught a fever,
She should work in the stinky sewers
And that's the best joke ever!
When she always smells of poo,
Which is funny and funky,
We just push her head down the loo,
Pop goes the Pooky!"

That song made all the children in school laugh, except for Donald and Douglas, Pooky's brothers, and Amrita, Pooky's best friend. They were shocked and angry, and they hated Hector and Rocky for being horrid and rude to Pooky.

The reason they kept bullying Pooky, is because, after she'd finished her meals or playing with her toys with her brothers in the playroom or doing her lessons at school, she felt her tummy rumble and then she did a little fart, which sounded like this:

Pppfffttt!

Afterwards, Pooky knew that she needed the toilet immediately. Luckily, she was fast and always managed to reach it just in time.

So that was why Hector and Rocky liked bullying her because she was a very special little girl.

And that was why poor Pooky felt very sad and upset and sometimes worried that nobody would like her. She really didn't like it when the two naughty boys played a dirty prank on her.

Well, let's start with Pooky and her brothers going to school, and we'll see what happens next.

Chapter 5
The Horrible Prank

One day, I think it was a Wednesday, Pooky, Donald and Douglas walked happily all the way to school. Amrita was going the same way and they chatted together as they walked along the pavement.

"I hope they won't pick on me while I'm doing my lessons," said Pooky, with a worried thought.

"Don't worry about them!" replied Donald. "We'll keep an eye on Hector and Rocky if they get up to their no-good tricks again."

"Exactly!" added Douglas. "We'll even ask the headmistress to keep watch on them too!"

"At least I'll be in class with you Pooky," said Amrita. She held onto Pooky's hand as they began to cross the road.

"I am so glad to have two big helpful brothers and a best friend like you!" Smiled Pooky. Soon, they arrived at the school just as the headmistress was ringing the bell and they went to their classrooms.

"We'll see you later at break time," said the twins as they went off to their class.

Pooky and Amrita went to Class 1. It was their favourite classroom because it was where they studied history.

Mrs Paige was their history teacher, and she was a very wise woman. She could teach history from the beginning of time right up to now. She was also a very kind person. If anyone had a problem or someone was causing trouble, she stepped in to fix it.

She particularly liked Pooky and Amrita because they behaved better than the other children, especially Hector and Rocky, who were in the same class.

Once all the children sat at their desks, Mrs Paige began the lesson.

"Good morning, boys and girls!" she said politely. "Today, we will be studying the 1500s."

Some of the children thought that was boring but Pooky and Amrita thought it was very exciting.

"Now then, after King Richard the Third was defeated in the Wars of the Roses who took over and became the new king of England?" asked Mrs Paige.

Pooky raised her hand gently and said politely, "Was it Henry the Seventh who became the new king of England?"

"Very good Pooky, well done!" replied the teacher. "Yes, it was Henry the Seventh who became king. Now, many years later in the 1500s, Queen Elizabeth the First always needed the toilet, but holes in the ground were not very suitable for a queen, so what did she have in her castle?" she asked.

Amrita answered, "Maybe she had one of the first famous flushing loos, Miss."

"Correct Amrita! She did have one of the first famous flushing loos!" Mrs Paige said. "That way, she could always use it whenever she wanted to," she added.

"Just like Smelly Poo!" Hector smirked.

"Yeah, she always smells of raw sewage!" added Rocky.

The children started laughing, but that made Mrs Paige cross. "Hector and Rocky! Stop bullying Pooky or you'll both be in detention!" she snapped.

Then she went around the room handing out workbooks to the children and returned to her desk. "Now children, I want to you to write down the words from the blackboard and then we'll study more about the Tudors," said Mrs Paige.

So, the children opened their books and started to write. Suddenly, as Pooky was writing the words down from the blackboard, she felt her tummy beginning to rumble and then pppffftttt!

"Oh no!" said Pooky as she crossed her legs tightly and struggled to carry on writing. Amrita was writing very neatly when she sniffed and then looked at Pooky.

"Are you OK?" she asked.

"I don't know, but I think I've got a runny tummy," Pooky whispered. Then she raised her hand and waited for Mrs Paige to come over.

Eventually, Mrs Paige saw that Pooky's hand was up and went to her. "What's wrong?" she asked.

"Sorry to call you over, Miss," she whispered, "but my tummy is rumbling, and I've farted by accident because I've a runny tummy." Then she added, "Please may I have your permission to go and use the toilet?"

"Yes of course you can, Pooky!" Mrs Paige smiled. "I'll escort you there immediately."

Mrs Paige helped Pooky out of her desk and took her to the door. As she opened the door she turned back to the children and said, "Children! I'm just going to escort Pooky to the toilets and I want no naughty pranks from any of you by the time I get back, especially you Hector and Rocky. Do I make myself clear?"

"Yes, Miss!" cried the children.

"Good! Now carry on with your work!" ordered Mrs Paige. She shut the door behind her and took Pooky down the corridor to the toilets. After they had gone, Hector said to Rocky, "OK, now's our chance to do a trick on Smelly Old Poo."

So, while no one was looking, the two naughty boys sneaked out of the classroom quietly and went to fetch a bucket of poo from the back of the toilets.

Pooky and Mrs Paige made it to the bathroom just in time.

"Right Pooky, you lift up your dress, while I sort out your tights and drawers," Mrs Paige said.

When they had done that, Pooky lifted the lid of the toilet and sat down very gently.

"Oh, that's better!" said Pooky as she sat comfortably. Then she lifted her head and looked at Mrs Paige and said, "Thanks for helping me, Miss. I'm sorry I had to ask you to escort me to the toilet."

"Oh, that's alright, Pooky. It's not your fault. Besides you did the right thing by telling me that you needed the toilet," replied Mrs Paige.

As Pooky sat, she became very sad.

"What's the matter dear?" the teacher asked.

"Well, you know about my problem and that everyone keeps making fun of me because I fart," she answered worriedly. "Sometimes I feel that I don't fit in at all," she added.

"Oh, cheer up!" Mrs Paige sighed. "You do fit in with the school because you're a good pupil and you've never done anything wrong in your life. There's nothing for you to worry about. I'll sort out those two boys out later."

This made Pooky feel a little better as she rubbed her tummy gently.

"Do you like rubbing your tummy?" asked Mrs Paige.

"Yes, it helps me to feel a lot better when I'm on the toilet or on my potty!" replied Pooky. At last, the rumbling stopped. "I've finished now, Miss! Will you help me wipe my bottom please?" she asked.

"Certainly!" Mrs Paige grinned. She grabbed some paper from the holder on the wall and began to clean Pooky's bottom while she held her dress up to her chest.

"There you are. All nice and clean again," the teacher said.

"Thank you, Miss. I'd better wash my hands," replied Pooky.

After she had washed and dried her hands they started to walk back to the classroom.

"You can go to your desk now and we'll have a talk with the headmistress later," said Mrs Paige.

"OK, Miss!"

Then there was trouble! As Pooky opened the door of the classroom, the bucket of poo that was sitting on top of the door, tipped over and landed right on top of Pooky with a big splat!

All the children laughed and laughed at this horrible prank, except for Amrita. She was shocked and horrified. So was Mrs Paige. Hector and Rocky you see, had loaded the bucket with poo from the back of the toilets and sneaked back into the classroom. They placed the bucket on the top of the door, then crept back to their desks, just as Pooky and Mrs Paige returned.

Pooky was so embarrassed, she burst into tears and began to cry.

"Holy gods! Who has put that bucket of poo on top of the door?" shouted Mrs Paige. She was absolutely furious. Then she noticed footprints on the floor and saw that the mud was from the shoes of Hector and Rocky.

"Hector and Rocky! How dare you play a horrible prank on poor Pooky! You horrid naughty boys!" bellowed Mrs Paige.

"Don't be stupid, it can't be us. We were at our desks the whole time," fibbed Hector.

"No, you weren't, because you've both got mud on the bottom of your shoes!" cried Mrs Paige. Rocky looked down and realised that she was right.

"I want you both to apologise to Pooky right now!" she demanded.

"What? No chance you silly old hag!" They smirked.

"I'm warning you! If you don't apologise right now, you'll both be in detention for the rest of the day!" snapped Mrs Paige. But the boys refused and pulled faces at her.

"Right, that's it! Go to the detention room now and you both can stay there for the rest of the day!"

So, Hector and Rocky walked out of the classroom to the detention room, and Mrs Paige said, "It's alright Pooky, let's get you washed. Amrita, please will you go and tell the headmistress what's happened while I get Pooky cleaned up?"

"Yes, Miss, right away!" said Amrita, and away she went to the headmistress' office.

Chapter 6
Miss Hurricane – the Headmistress

Amrita went to see the headmistress. She was very cross that the naughty boys weren't being nice to Pooky. "I hope she'll know what to do," she said thoughtfully. Soon she arrived at the headmistress's office and knocked quietly on the door.

"Come in!" cried a voice from inside the office. Amrita opened the door, walked in slowly and closed the door behind her.

"Hello, Miss Hurricane!" she said.

Miss Hurricane was a very big and kind woman. She loved helping the children when there was trouble in the school. She had big strong hands and she had a whip with her, just in case anyone was being naughty.

"Oh, hello Amrita. How can I help you?" asked Miss Hurricane.

Amrita sat down on a chair and began to explain what had happened.

"Well, Miss, it's about Pooky. You see, Hector and Rocky have played a horrible prank on her by placing a bucket of poo on top of the door. When she came back from the bathroom with Mrs Paige, Pooky opened the door and the bucket tipped over and landed on her. I was really shocked that she was covered all over in poo and felt very sorry for her."

"I see!" said the headmistress. "Was she hurt?"

"Well, she felt very hurt and upset by that naughty prank."

Miss Hurricane agreed. "You did the right thing by coming to explain about what happened. Where are the boys now?" she asked.

"Mrs Paige sent them to the detention room after they refused to apologise, and Pooky has gone to get washed and cleaned up."

The headmistress thought for a moment, then said to Amrita, "Thank you for coming to see me. You can go back to class now and I'll try and think what to with those horrid naughty boys."

As Amrita set off back to class, the headmistress turned to her advisor and said, "Mrs Walden, would you get on the phone to Pooky's parents please?"

"Yes, Miss, straight away!" said Mrs Walden. She was Miss Hurricane's advisor and assistant. She was very sensible lady and liked to keep herself busy. She picked up the telephone and rang the operator.

"Hello, can you put me through to Mr and Mrs Beaumont of house number six, Holland Park Avenue, London please?" asked Mrs Walden. The operator accepted Mrs Walden's request and began to put her through to the Beaumonts at once.

At home, Penelope was in her study sorting out the paperwork for the councillor, when the telephone rang. Ring! Ring! Ring! Ring! "I'll get it!" cried Igor in a slowly warming voice and answered the phone.

Chapter 7
The Shock

"Hello! Igor speaking!"

"Hello!" said Mrs Walden. "This is Mrs Walden from Victorian School. Please may I speak to Mrs Beaumont? It's about her daughter!"

"Certainly, Ma'am!" said Igor. "Hold on please." He put the phone down on the table, then went to Penelope's study and knocked at the door. Knock! Knock! Knock!

"Come in!" called Penelope.

Igor opened the door and walked in. "Sorry to bother you, M'lady, but Mrs Walden is on the phone. She wants to speak to you about Pooky!" explained Igor.

Penelope was surprised, then went out of her study and picked up the phone. "Hello Mrs Walden," said Penelope. "Is there anything wrong?"

"I'll put you on to Miss Hurricane and she'll explain what has happened," replied Mrs Walden.

She then handed the phone over to the headmistress. "Mrs Beaumont is on the phone now, Miss," she said.

"Thank you!" said Miss Hurricane.

"Hello, Mrs Beaumont. Sorry to trouble you, but I want to speak to you about your daughter," began the headmistress.

"Why? What has happened to her?"

"Well, the two naughty boys, Hector and Rocky, have played a horrible prank. They put a bucket full of poo on top of the classroom door and when Pooky opened the door, the bucket tipped over and landed right on top of Pooky, covering her all over in poo!"

Mrs Beaumont was shocked.

"Oh, my goodness! Was she hurt?"

"No, she's alright," answered Miss Hurricane, "but she is really upset, and Mrs Paige has gone to get her washed and cleaned up."

Then she added, "When she is washed and cleaned, I'll get Mrs Walden to bring Pooky home for you."

"That's very kind of you!" said Penelope.

"My pleasure." Miss Hurricane smiled. "When she has had a good rest, she'll be alright for school again tomorrow," she added.

"Well, thank you for letting me know" – Penelope sighed – "I'll take care of my daughter and see if I can cheer up. Goodbye!" Then she put the phone down and began to feel worried. *Oh, my poor little girl! Those horrid boys must be stopped as soon as possible,* she thought. Then she rang the police.

"Hello! Police Sergeant Arnold Nesbit speaking," said the sergeant.

"Hello, Arnold, it's me, Penelope Beaumont."

"Oh, hello Penelope, how are you?" asked Arnold.

"Very well, thank you, but I do have a very big problem."

Arnold looked puzzled, then said, "What's the problem?"

"It's my daughter, Pooky. She was being bullied and teased by Hector and Rocky," replied Mrs Beaumont, and she began to tell him what Miss Hurricane had said.

"I see!" Arnold sighed. "Don't worry! I'll make sure we'll keep an eye on those two horrid naughty boys."

Penelope smiled and said, "Thank you Arnold. See you soon!" Then she put the phone and went back to the study to finish off the paperwork before Pooky came home.

Chapter 8
Cleaning Pooky

A little while later, Mrs Walden arrived at the Beaumonts house with Pooky. She rang the bell and waited patiently.

"Am I in trouble, Miss?" asked Pooky sadly.

"Oh no, Pooky. Of course, you're not in trouble." Mrs Walden smiled. "Besides, it really wasn't your fault at all, it was all Hector and Rocky's fault!"

Just then the door opened, and Penelope came out. "Hello, Mummy!" said Pooky as she wept with tears.

"Oh, you poor girl!" replied her mother. "You go upstairs to the bathroom and try not to worry about today, sweetheart! Mitzi and Sophie have got the bath ready for you," she added.

Pooky dried her tears and went upstairs to the bathroom. "See you tomorrow, Mrs Walden," she said as she waved goodbye.

"Yes, see you tomorrow Pooky. Goodbye!" called Mrs Walden.

"Thanks for bringing her home, Mrs Walden," Penelope said.

"It's my pleasure!" she replied. "Something will be done about those boys; they're just causing trouble for Pooky."

"I hope so." Penelope sighed.

"Well, I'd better head back. Miss Hurricane will be wondering where I am," murmured Mrs Walden. Then she waved goodbye to Penelope and set off back to the school.

After Mrs Walden left and Penelope closed the door, Mitzi came downstairs to speak to her. "We've managed to get the rest of the poo off Pooky, Ma'am, and while Sophie is helping her, I'll get her clothes washed and ask Remy to make a warm drink of hot cocoa."

"Excellent! Carry on, I'm just going up to see how she's doing," she said quietly.

She went upstairs to the bathroom and knocked on the door. Knock! Knock! Knock!

"Come in, Madam!" called Sophie. Penelope opened the door and went in. Sophie was drying Pooky's hair, as she sat down on a chair with a warm towel wrapped around her.

"How are you feeling now, sweetheart?" asked her mother.

"I feel all nice and clean again, Mummy!" replied Pooky. Then she felt a bit sleepy and yawned.

"You sound tired, dear," said Penelope as she stroked her daughter. "Why don't I help you into your nightie and you can have a nice nap?" she added.

Pooky thought that was a good idea. After she was dry, Penelope took her into the bedroom.

She helped Pooky into her nightie and then she climbed into her bed. Mitzi came in with mug of warm cocoa.

"This will help you feel better," said Mitzi. "It always works!"

"Thanks Mitzi," said Pooky, and drank the cocoa very slowly. After she had finished, she said, "I think I'll have my nap now!"

"OK, sweetie! I'll wake you up later at about six o'clock," said Penelope, and then she kissed her on her forehead. Penelope and Mitzi walked out of the room and closed the door behind them. Pooky laid down on her pillow, hugged her favourite teddy bear, closed her eyes and was soon fast asleep.

Chapter 9
Amrita Comes to Dinner

Later, at 5.45 pm, Jack and the boys returned home for the day.

"Hello darling," said Jack. "Did you have a nice day sorting out the paperwork?"

"Yes Jack, and how about you boys, did you have a lovely day at school?" asked Penelope.

"Oh, yes, Mum, we did," exclaimed Donald.

"But then we found out what had happened to Pooky from her best friend, Amrita," said Douglas.

They added, "We have invited Amrita and her family around join us for dinner tonight and they were pleased about that."

"Well, I'd better tell Igor to add three more chairs." Penelope smiled.

Igor, who was standing in the dining room, said, "No need, lady, I'm on it!" And went to the store cupboard to get three more chairs.

"How is she, love?" asked Jack.

"Oh, she's fine! She's asleep in her bedroom. I'm just going to wake her up now," she replied.

Penelope went upstairs to check on Pooky. She opened the door and walked in quietly, sat down beside her and sighed with a smile. *She is very sweet and beautiful*, she thought, *I just wish I could make her life a lot better*. Then she put her hand on Pooky's shoulder and gave a gentle shake.

Pooky woke up, stretched and sat up in bed. "Oh, hi, Mummy." She yawned.

"Hello dear, did you have a wonderful nap?" her mother asked.

"Yes, I did thanks," said Pooky, scratching her head.

"Your best friend, Amrita, and her family are coming around to dinner tonight," announced Penelope. "I'll help you into your fresh clothes, then we can go downstairs and wait for them." Pooky was excited. She got out of bed, took off her nightie and began to decide what to wear for the evening. Soon, she was wearing a beautiful dress. It was of sparkling gold, with a silver petticoat and a clean white apron around it.

They walked downstairs and into the dining room where Jack and the boys were sitting at the table talking.

"Hello, Poppet," said Jack. "Did you have a nice rest?"

"Hello, Daddy. I certainly did!" replied Pooky, then she calmly sat down at the table just as the doorbell rang. Ding dong!

Igor went to answer the door. He opened it, and on the step, stood Amrita and her parents, Mr and Mrs Desai.

"Good evening. You must be Amrita Desai, is that correct?" asked Igor.

"Good evening. Yes, that's right!" replied Amrita.

"We're here for dinner with the Beaumonts," said Mr Desai.

"Donald and Douglas invited us," added Mrs Desai.

"Indeed, right this way if you please!" replied Igor and took them to the dining room where the family were waiting.

Igor walked in and announced, "Mr and Mrs Desai are here with their daughter, Miss Amrita."

Everyone greeted each other and the guests were made welcome. Soon, they were all sitting around the table. Amrita sat next to Pooky so she could keep her company.

"Are you OK now?" she asked.

"Yes!" answered Pooky.

Mr and Mrs Desai had a nice chat with her. "Amrita told us about those two horrid naughty boys," spluttered Mr Desai.

"It's not fair for them to be so horrid to you," muttered Mrs Desai.

Amrita placed her hand on Pooky's and said, "We're all very sorry for you."

Pooky give her a small smile and a big hug.

Remy the cook walked in and happily said, "Dinner is served!" Mitzi and Sophie followed with a big trolley full of lots of food.

They enjoyed the delicious meal of roast beef with roast potatoes, Yorkshire puddings and vegetables. They had funny chats and told stories about their day.

After they finished their meals, Remy came back with a big dish of spotted dick for dessert, along with a bowl of custard.

As they ate, Mr Desai said to Jack, "Have you heard the news from the market today?"

"No! Why?" asked Jack.

"Well, people in the market are getting poorly because the food has gone rotten and smells awful," Mr Desai replied.

"That sounds terrible!" cried Donald and Douglas. "Who would do such a thing as that?"

"I don't know, but whoever caused this trouble will be caught and punished!" snapped Mr Desai.

Pooky and Amrita didn't like this, but they just said nothing.

Later that evening, it was time for the Desai family to go home. "Thank you for inviting us," they said. "It has been a wonderful night dining with you!"

"You're quite welcome!" said Mr Beaumont.

"Do come again any time you like."

"See you tomorrow, Pooky," said Amrita.

Pooky waved goodbye to her friend and her parents until they were out of sight. "Well, that was a wonderful evening!" said Penelope.

"It really was darling!" replied Jack. Then the clock on the wall struck nine o'clock.

"Right. It's bedtime now, kids," said Penelope. The children gave their parents a warm hug and climbed up the stairs to bed.

"Good night, Pooky," said Jack. "Let's hope it's a better day for you tomorrow."

"I hope so too." Pooky sighed. "Well, good night then!"

"Good night, sweetheart!" replied Penelope. Then she said to her husband, "Let's go to bed too. We can only hope that nothing will go wrong tomorrow."

Jack thought that this was a good idea, so they said goodnight to Igor, Mitzi and Sophie and went upstairs to bed.

Chapter 10
Pooky in Trouble

The next morning, the sun was shining brightly and everyone in the house was up and ready for another busy day. Pooky was the first to wake and put on her clothes, ready for school.

Donald and Douglas also got ready. They cleaned and dressed each other to make themselves look smart and handsome for school as well.

Soon, they all went downstairs and sat at the table to wait for their breakfast.

"Morning Donald and Douglas!" said Pooky.

"Morning Pooky. Are you feeling OK now?" they asked.

"Absolutely!" she replied.

Just then, Mr and Mrs Beaumont came into the dining room ready for breakfast as well. "Good morning children!" said Jack. "Lovely day today."

"It really is, Dad," said Donald.

"Just the day to do studying," added Douglas.

In came Mitzi and Sophie with the big trolley of porridge, toast, and other tasty things.

Pooky loved eating porridge. It was her favourite breakfast meal, especially with some sugar on top.

Soon they finished their breakfast and the children cleared up their bowls and plates, loaded them onto the trolley and went upstairs to clean their teeth. When they had finished, they picked up their school bags and went downstairs to say goodbye.

"Goodbye!" said Penelope. "Have a good day at school and we'll see you later."

"See you later, Mum, bye!" cried the twins.

"Goodbye!" said Pooky and they walked along the road to school together.

Arriving at the school gates, they saw that Amrita was already there. "Morning everyone!" she called. "Let's hope everything is going to be fine," she added with a sigh. They went to their classrooms and sat at their desks ready to begin lessons.

"Morning class! Today we'll be studying about the Stuart times," said Mrs Paige.

"Is it in the Stuart times that Guy Fawkes tried to blow up the king on the 5th of November, Miss?" asked Pooky.

"Yes, correct Pooky!" Mrs Paige replied. "And after Guy Fawkes failed to blow the king up, Evil Oliver Cromwell took over the whole of Great Britain," she added.

"Excuse me, Miss, but didn't Oliver Cromwell ban Christmas, theatre and sports?" Amrita asked.

"Yes, that's right! He didn't think they were fun at all!" Mrs Paige said.

Hector and Rocky smirked and said, "Well, Smelly Poo is fun!" The children laughed.

"No, don't be silly. Smelly Poo is not fun, it is horrible and not nice at all!" snapped Mrs Paige. "And I don't want any silly questions, thank you very much," she added.

Later, it was break time, and the children went outside to play. Mrs Paige went to speak to Pooky and Amrita. "Excellent work in class girls," she said. "You go out and play now and afterwards, we'll carry on learning more from the Stuart times."

Pooky and Amrita went off to play. On the way, Amrita said, "I just need to go to the play cupboard and get some skipping ropes. You wait here and I'll be back in a minute."

So, while Amrita went to the play cupboard, Pooky waited on a chair in the corridor. Just then, Hector and Rocky came down the corridor, ready for causing mischief. "Oh look, it's Smelly Poo." Hector smirked.

"Yeah, doesn't she smell awful!" Rocky laughed.

This made Pooky embarrassed, but she said nothing.

"You're not so special, are you?" The boys snorted.

Pooky turned to the boys and said politely, "Everyone is special and there no need to bully someone who is absolutely special. Besides, every child in this school is special."

The boys laughed at this comment and then Hector said, "Nonsense, Poo, there's nothing special about any of it. In fact, you could just stick your own head down the toilet!" And that's what gave the two horrid boys a very naughty idea.

"Now that you mention it, let's stick her head down the toilet. Grab her!" shouted Rocky. They both got hold of Pooky's arms and dragged her all the way to the toilet.

"Noooo!" shouted Pooky. "Please let me go!"

But the boys ignored her, and they pulled her into the bathroom.

"Lift up the lid, Rocky!" ordered Hector, and Rocky flipped the lid up and they pulled Pooky to the hole of the toilet.

"Please stop it, stop it!" Pooky shouted, but still the boys paid no attention to her.

"Now, let's see how you like it!" Rocky smirked, and they began to push her head into the hole of the toilet and her face was covered from her hair to her neck in brown smelly poo.

Outside the bathroom, Donald and Douglas were quietly talking in the corridor. "I think studying is great fun, Douglas," said Donald.

"I quite agree, Donald," replied Douglas. Just as they were about to pass the bathroom, they heard a crying noise, "Owww! please, stop it!"

"Did you hear that?" asked Donald.

"I did!" cried Douglas. "It's coming from the bathroom."

They opened the door a tiny crack, looked in and saw Hector and Rocky pushing Pooky's head down the toilet and pulling her up again. "Please stop it! You're hurting me!" cried Pooky in tears.

Donald and Douglas gasped.

"Paint me pink!" whispered Donald. "Hector and Rocky are pushing Pooky down the toilet and now she's in trouble!"

"Yes," whispered Douglas. "What can we do to save our sister?"

Donald thought for a minute and then said quietly, "Go and fetch Mrs Paige and tell her what's happening. I'll stay here and keep watch."

"Good idea!" whispered Douglas and he ran off to find Mrs Paige while Donald kept watch on the boys.

Mrs Paige was sorting out the history books when Douglas rushed in.

"Hello Mrs Paige, sorry to bother you, but there's an emergency," he said breathlessly.

"Emergency? What's happened?" asked Mrs Paige.

"It's Pooky! Hector and Rocky are pushing her head down the toilet in the bathroom and covering her head in poo," explained Douglas. Mrs Paige was horrified.

"Are they still there?" she asked.

"Yes, Donald is keeping watch," Douglas answered.

"Come on then, lead the way," ordered Mrs Paige, and she began to run behind Douglas as they sped to the bathroom.

Outside the bathroom, Donald was still keeping watch when Douglas and Mrs Paige turned up.

"Ah, Donald, are they in there now?" asked Mrs Paige.

"Yes, Miss, they're still in there!" replied Donald.

"Right, stand back. I'm going in!" said Mrs Paige. She burst the door open and ran straight into the bathroom shouting, "Hector and Rocky! Stop pushing Pooky down the toilet right now!"

Hector and Rocky jumped backwards and landed on their backs with a bump. Mrs Paige was absolutely furious. "Both of you wash your hands and wait outside the bathroom now!" she shouted, and the boys quickly washed their hands and then they went outside to wait.

Mrs Paige went over to Pooky and pulled her out of the toilet gently.

"Are you alright?" she asked.

"I'm alright, but my head is covered in poo." Pooky sobbed.

"It's a good thing your big brothers told me what was happening." Mrs Paige smiled, then she turned and spoke to the twins, "Will you go and get a bucket of warm water, scrubbing brush and a towel please?"

"Of course, Miss," said Donald and Douglas, and they went to get the stuff.

Just then Amrita came into the bathroom and gasped with shock. "Oh, my goodness. What happened?" she asked.

"Hector and Rocky have gone too far this time," said Mrs Paige. "They pushed Pooky down the toilet and she's covered in poo."

Then she added, "Can you look after her while I take these two naughty boys to the headmistress's office?"

"Yes, Miss," Amrita replied.

While Amrita kept Pooky company, Mrs Paige angrily took Hector and Rocky to Miss Hurricane's office.

Chapter 11
The Stern Talk

Miss Hurricane was busy in her office with Mrs Walden when there was a loud knock at the door. Knock! Knock! Knock!

"Come in!" she called. Mrs Paige opened the door and dragged Hector and Rocky into the room. "Ah, Mrs Paige, what have these boys done now?" she asked.

"Well, Miss Hurricane," said Mrs Paige crossly. "Hector and Rocky have gone too far this time. They dragged poor Pooky to the bathroom, opened the lid of the toilet and then they pushed her head down and she was covered in poo."

"What? Pushed her head down the toilet?" shouted Miss Hurricane.

"Yes, Miss. Luckily, Donald and Douglas managed to tell me, and I've stopped them!"

Miss Hurricane stood up and said, "Thank you Mrs Paige, I'll take over." And she gave a stern talk to the horrid boys. "Hector and Rocky! You two have been causing a lot of trouble and mischief and you both are very, very, very, very naughty."

"But she started it, Miss," protested Hector. "She was the one who caused the trou—"

"Don't lie to me!" snapped Miss Hurricane. "I've been headmistress of the Victorian School for twenty years and I've never been so furious in all my life!" Then she added, "You have been very horrid to Pooky. You've been teasing her, you've been calling her rude names, you've been abusing her and this time, you've been hurting her. I really have had quite enough of your naughty tricks and pranks and now, I have no choice but to say that you two are both expelled!"

"Rubbish! You can't be serious?" said Rocky.

"Oh, actually I am very serious, because I am always serious and very stern and, like I said, you two are both expelled!" boomed Miss Hurricane.

This made Hector and Rocky very cross, but before they could protest, Miss Hurricane turned to Mrs Walden and said, "Will you help the boys to gather their belongings together and then take them home please?"

"Yes, Miss Hurricane!" she answered and took the boys out of the office to get their belongings. As they walked to the classroom, they went past Donald, Douglas and Amrita who were in the bathroom helping Pooky to wash her face and hair.

"She'll pay for this!" they whispered furiously. When they had their belongings, Mrs Walden took the two boys out of the school.

When Donald, Douglas and Amrita had finished cleaning Pooky's face and hair, Pooky looked out of the window and saw Mrs Walden taking Hector and Rocky away.

"Well, at least you will never ever see them again," Amrita said.

"I hope so." Pooky sighed with a little worry.

Chapter 12
The Midnight Talk

When school was over, Pooky, Donald and Douglas waved goodbye to Amrita and set off for home. Soon, they arrived and went inside. While Pooky went upstairs to get herself cleaned again, Donald and Douglas went to find their mum. They found her sitting in the living room sorting through the sheets of documents for the councillor.

"Hello boys! How was school today?" asked Penelope.

"It went well, thanks, Mum," said Donald. "We've got something to tell you," added Douglas. They sat down next to her and began to tell her what had happened at the school. "Hector and Rocky have gone too far this time!" they said.

"What do you mean?" Penelope asked, puzzled.

"Well, they dragged Pooky all the way to toilet, lifted the lid and pushed her down the toilet. Her face was covered in poo, and she was very upset."

"Oh, my poor baby! Is she alright?" cried Penelope panicking.

"Oh, yes, she's alright, Mum!" said Donald. "She's gone upstairs to get herself cleaned up and then she is going to read a book in the playroom."

Douglas said, "We managed to tell Mrs Paige that Pooky was in trouble, and she saved her from the horrid naughty boys, and Miss Hurricane has expelled them from the Victorian School. So, that way, Pooky won't have to worry about them."

"Thank you for telling me that boys, and well done for going to Mrs Walden and telling her about it," said Penelope. "I'm glad those boys won't be around to bully her anymore."

That night, everyone was fast asleep in bed. Pooky had also been asleep, feeling tired after what happened at school. Suddenly, she woke up after a little fart blew right out of her bottom. Pppffftt!

"Oh no, not again!" cried Pooky. She quickly jumped out of bed and grabbed her potty from under the bed. She put it down by the front of the bedside leg, lifted her nightie up and sat down on the potty softly.

"Oh, that's better!" she said with sigh, and as she sat on the potty, the poo came plopping out of her bottom.

Plop! Plop! Plop! Pft! Then she thought about the day at school, she thought about the boys bullying and teasing her and she thought about the children laughing at her. She thought about that so much that she burst into tears and began to cry.

"I just don't understand why all the children in school make fun of me." Pooky sobbed, and she cried even louder.

In her parents' bedroom above her, Jack and Penelope were asleep when the sound of crying woke Penelope up.

I wonder who is crying? she thought to herself. So, she got out of bed and put on her shawl and slippers. She lit a candle and went out of the room to find out where the crying was coming from.

Penelope went to Donald and Douglas's bedroom door and listened, but there was no sound. "Well, it's not them." She sighed and went downstairs to Pooky's bedroom.

When she got there, she pressed her ear to Pooky's door and listened. That was where crying was coming from. She opened the door a tiny crack and looked in. She saw Pooky sitting on the potty and crying wet tears. Penelope was more worried than ever, so she walked into her daughter's bedroom quietly. Pooky looked up and saw her mother coming into her room.

"Hello, Mummy!" said Pooky as a tear rolled down her cheek.

"Hello, sweetheart! Are you crying?" she asked.

"Yes! I'm very upset about everything at school, and I am very tired and lonely," she added.

Penelope put the candle on the chest of drawers and sat down next to her to keep her company.

"It's alright, dear! It's alright, I'm here!" replied her mother. "Donald and Douglas told me about what happened today and I'm glad that you're alright. It was very brave of your brothers to save you from Hector and Rocky." She handed Pooky her handkerchief so she could dry her eyes. "Do you know, I felt the same when I was your age love," she said as she hugged her.

Suddenly, Pooky stopped crying, surprised. "Really?" she asked.

"Yes," Penelope said. "You see, when I was young, all the children at school used to bully me and pick on me. They even said rude names, calling me Pee, because they thought I smelled of wee!"

"Gosh, that's terrible!" cried Pooky.

"It was!" Penelope sighed. "And they even played pranks on me by putting a bucket of wee on top of the classroom door and when I opened the door to go in, the bucket tipped and landed on me, and I was covered all over in wee!"

Pooky was surprised. "So, what did you do after they made fun of you?" she asked.

"Well, after two days, I stood up to them and explained that I am proud of who I am and I said that I was as special as any child and I also said that if they kept on bullying me, I would bully them back and they stopped after that," explained Penelope.

This made Pooky feel better. "Did you tell the teachers about the bullying?" she asked.

"Yes, I did!" went on Penelope. "And they managed to sort the problem out for me!"

She gave her daughter a small smile and then said, "So, you see sweetheart, when someone is bullying you or abusing you, you need to take a deep breath and stand up to them by telling them how very special you are and how proud you are too, then they'll stop bullying you and leave you to get on with your life."

Pooky was so touched by her mother's story that her tummy began to feel better.

"Have you finished on your potty, dear?" asked Penelope.

"Yes, Mummy, I have!" she answered.

"I'll go and get you a roll of toilet paper."

Penelope said and went to the bathroom to get one. After two minutes, she came back carrying the toilet paper. Then she cleaned Pooky's bottom and put a sheet of brown paper over the potty to stop the smell coming out, then she took her to the bathroom so that Pooky could wash her hands. When that was done, Penelope took her back to bed.

As Pooky laid down on her bed, she said, "I think that was a funny story about your life, Mummy."

"It really was, dear!" said her mother, as she stroked her hair gently. "You've been through a horrible time sweetheart," she said. "Why don't you stay here tomorrow? You can sleep on the sofa in the playroom, and I can spend time with you when I've finished my paperwork for the councillor."

"Thanks, Mummy, I would like that!" said Pooky sleepily.

"Good! I'll ask the twins to explain to Miss Hurricane that you're staying here tomorrow," said Penelope. Then she kissed her on her head very softly.

"Good night, Mummy," replied Pooky, then she closed her eyes and fell asleep.

"Good night, dear," Penelope said as she picked up her candle, went out of Pooky's room and closed the door behind her.

"I'm glad that story made her feel better!" Penelope smiled, and then she climbed back up the stairs to bed.

Chapter 13
Looking After Pooky

The next morning, Jack and Penelope woke up to a bright sunny day and sat up in bed. "Morning love, you've slept alright?" asked Penelope.

"Morning dear, I have! How about you?" Jack replied.

Penelope began to tell Jack about what happed last night. "I woke up in the middle of the night and heard someone crying," she said, "so, I went to see who and found out that it was Pooky."

"Was she upset about the bullies?" asked Jack.

"She was!" she said. "I sat down beside her and told her that I was bullied in the same way. She felt a lot better when she heard about my life story." She went on, "I'm going to phone the school after breakfast to tell them that Pooky is staying here today."

"I think that's a kind idea, dear," said Jack.

"Anyway, I'd better get myself ready for work." They got out of bed and went to their bathroom to get themselves cleaned and dressed.

Soon, everyone in the house woke and got dressed ready to start the day. Pooky woke up last but kept her nightie on so she could have a nice rest in the playroom. She went to the bathroom to wash her face. When she finished, she went downstairs to the dining room with her favourite teddy bear and waited. Soon her parents and brothers came into the dining room for breakfast.

"Morning Poppet, you OK?" asked Jack.

"Yeah, I'm OK, Daddy!" said Pooky as she sat. Penelope explained to Donald and Douglas that Pooky was going to stay at home today.

"Will you let Amrita and the teachers know for me boys?" she said.

"We will, Mum," replied the twins.

Remy, Igor, and the housemaids came in with breakfast on the trolley and, when everything was laid, the family began to eat. When the porridge and toast with jam and honey was finished, they cleared the table, put the breakfast things back onto the trolley and took them to the kitchen to get them washed and cleaned.

Pooky said to Donald and Douglas, "You two can use the bathroom first and I'll go in after you."

"Thank you, Pooky," said Donald.

"That's very kind of you," added Douglas, and they went upstairs to clean their teeth.

Pooky got off her chair and went to sit on her mother's lap. "Do you think I'm alright resting in the playroom, Mummy?" she asked.

"I certainly hope so, sweetie!" Penelope answered. "Now, you go and clean your teeth and I'll bring your potty into the playroom," she added.

Jack went over and kissed Pooky on the cheek. "See you tonight, dear!" he said.

Pooky got down from her mother's lap, kissed her dad goodbye and went upstairs with her teddy bear to clean her teeth. A few minutes later, she came back downstairs with her bear and went into the playroom where Penelope was waiting.

"I've brought your potty and a roll of toilet paper down just in case if you have a runny tummy again," said Penelope.

"Thanks, Mummy," Pooky said quietly.

Then Mitzi and Sophie came in with Pooky's pillow and quilt.

"We thought you might need these," said Mitzi, and they began to make her feel comfortable on the sofa.

"Thanks ladies!" she replied, then she closed her eyes, laid her head down on her pillow and went to sleep.

Penelope stroked Pooky's hair gently and smiled.

"Have a good rest, dear!" she whispered. Then she turned to Mitzi and Sophie and said, "Let's leave her and we'll take it in turns checking on her after one hour each."

"Of course, Ma'am," said Sophie, and they walked out of the playroom very gently and quietly closed the door behind them.

Chapter 14
A Visit from the Doctor

Penelope went to her study to finish the paperwork and then send it to Spencer Perceval, who also worked for the councillor and the Prime Minister. She was half-way through sorting out the documents when she felt a kick in her tummy.

Hmm! she thought. *I think I'd better get the doctor to check me over to see if there's anything wrong with the baby inside me.*

You see, Penelope, I forgot to mention to you, was going to have a new baby and has kept it a secret from Pooky. She thought that Pooky would like a little baby brother or sister to play with after everything that she'd been through.

She called for Igor to come into her study.

Igor arrived and asked, "You called, M'lady?"

"Yes Igor! Would you telephone Dr Devonport and ask him to come and see me please? I just need a check-up," she said.

"Very good, M'lady. I'll phone him right away!" Igor said with a smile and went to telephone the doctor.

Wallace Devonport was an excellent doctor and he managed to help people all over the City of London feel a lot better. He made them well again when they caught chickenpox, a cold or a flu. He was in the study sorting out his schedule book when the telephone rang. Ring! Ring! Ring! Ring!

Answering it, he said, "Hello, Dr Devonport speaking!"

"Hello, Doctor, this is Igor, the Beaumonts' butler calling. Could you come to number six, Holland Park Avenue, please?" Igor asked. "It's just M'lady Penelope feels that she needs a check-up," he added.

The doctor looked through his schedule book to see if he had any appointments available, then spoke to Igor. "Well, luckily I have nothing in the schedule book today, so I'll be over there in twenty minutes."

"Splendid! See you shortly!" replied Igor, then he put the phone down and went to tell Penelope.

"Dr Devonport will be here in twenty minutes, Ma'am," Igor announced.

"Thanks Igor, you can go and have your break now," said Penelope.

Igor bowed gently and went back to his room to read his morning newspaper. Twenty minutes later, Dr Devonport arrived at the house and knocked on the door. Knock! Knock! Knock!

Igor went to open the door. "Hello Igor, I've come to give Penelope a check-up," said the doctor.

"Of course, come in!" Igor replied and showed Dr Devonport to Penelope's study. Penelope had just finished sorting out the paperwork when Igor came in.

"Dr Devonport is here, Adam!" he announced.

"Excellent, show him in," said Penelope. Igor led the doctor into the study.

"Hello Mrs Beaumont, I understand that you need a check-up to see if the baby inside you OK is, is that right?" Dr Devonport asked.

"Yes, that's right!" she replied. "Let's go to the living room and we'll get started."

Penelope and Igor led Dr Devonport to the living room. When they got there, Penelope laid on the sofa and relaxed so that the doctor could check the baby.

Dr Devonport put his stethoscope to his ears and listened to the heartbeat inside Penelope's tummy.

"Is there anything wrong, Doctor?" asked Penelope nervously. The doctor put his stethoscope away and smiled.

"No, Madam, your baby's heart is still beating nicely!" Dr Devonport replied.

"Oh, what a relief!" Penelope sighed, then sat up gently.

As the doctor popped his stethoscope back into his bag he asked, "Oh, by the way, how's your daughter, Pooky?"

"She's fine. She is asleep in the playroom," Penelope said. "I thought that she could do with a rest after all the trouble that Hector and Rocky put her through." Penelope added, "I'll show you." Then she led Dr Devonport to the playroom and opened the door a tiny crack. They looked in and saw Pooky still fast asleep on the sofa.

"Oh yes, I see what you mean!" whispered Dr Devonport. "Does she have any problems?" he asked.

"Well, she does have a runny tummy. You see, after she has her meals, or while she is playing with her toys or doing her homework, she feels her tummy rumbling and then she farts by accident."

"How long has that been going on?" asked Dr Devonport.

"About four years, I think," said Penelope, "and she feels very upset about it."

Dr Devonport thought for a few minutes, then he said, "Well, let's see how it goes for the next two months and if she still has a runny tummy then bring her to the hospital so we can do an operation on her. Is that OK with you?"

Penelope thought for a moment, she looked at Pooky, then she spoke to him, "Yes, that will be alright with me!"

"Splendid! Well, I'd better get back to my office," said Dr Devonport, and they shook hands. "Goodbye Mrs Beaumont, see you soon!" the doctor cried.

"Goodbye, Dr Devonport!" replied Penelope.

Then the doctor set off back to his office and Igor closed the door. "Was everything OK, M'lady?" he asked.

"Yes Igor, everything is OK!" Smiled Penelope. "Let's go and have a drink!"

Chapter 15
Spending Time with Pooky

Penelope and Igor went to the kitchen to get a drink of lemonade. They kindly asked Remy to join them.

"I'd be honoured!" he said. Remy went to get some glasses and a bottle of lemonade from the storage room.

Then they sat down and drank the cool bubbling lemonade. As they drank, Penelope said to herself, "I think I'll spend some time with Pooky." So, when they finished drinking, Penelope said to Igor and Remy, "I'm going to spend time with my daughter! Would you bring some bowls of warm tomato soup and bread for our lunch please?"

"Of course, Ma'am!" said Igor.

"I'll have it ready for lunchtime!" added Remy. Then Penelope went to the playroom to spend her time with Pooky. In the playroom, Pooky was still asleep and dreaming about her wonderful family. Then the door opened, and Penelope walked in carefully. She sat down on the sofa and gave Pooky a gentle shake. Pooky woke up slowly, yawned, stretched, and sat up on the sofa.

"Hello, darling. Did you have a good rest?" she asked.

"Very well indeed, Mummy!" replied Pooky.

She gave her a big hug and said, "I have finished the paperwork for the councillor now so I can spend time with you."

Pooky was pleased.

"Shall I read you a story?" Penelope asked.

"Yes, please, Mummy. I would like the book of Aesop's Fables, please!" Pooky requested. So Penelope went across the room to the bookshelf and picked up Aesop's Fables and sat back down on the sofa.

Pooky snuggled up close to her mother as she read, then they played with Pooky's toys. After that, they had some bowls of warm tomato soup and bread for lunch along with a bottle of lemonade to drink.

After lunch, they played with Pooky's lovely dolls and soon, it was three o'clock. Pooky and Penelope were very tired, but happy.

"I really enjoyed today, Mummy," declared Pooky as she hugged her teddy bear.

"Me too, sweetheart, me too!" replied Penelope. Jack, Donald, and Douglas returned home from a very busy day. Pooky and Penelope went to the door to greet them.

"Hello Pooky," said the twins. "How are you feeling now?"

"I feel much better, thanks!" replied Pooky, and she began to tell her brothers about the wonderful day she'd had.

"Well, it sounds like you both had fun!" said Jack. They all went into the living room and chatted for a while.

"While I was on my way home," said Jack, "I saw one of the people in the market who had been poisoned, and I think that Mr Desai was right. All the food at the market was rotten. It smelled awful and horrible!" he explained.

"Does anyone know who's causing all the trouble?" asked Penelope.

"No, my dear!" answered Jack. "But one of them said that there was something odd going on around there and they thought that it must come from somewhere that we didn't know about," he added.

"Anyway, let's go and have our dinner!" announced Jack. "All this talk of food is making my mouth water."

Everyone agreed and set off to the dining room to have dinner.

Chapter 16
Pooky and Percy

A few days later, Pooky was back at school with her best friend, Amrita, and, although she was glad that Hector and Rocky were not there to bully her anymore, she was a bit worried that they might go back to abuse her again.

Mrs Paige came into the classroom to start the day's work. "Morning class!" she said. "I hope you've had a good weekend!" Then she turned to Pooky and said, "Good to have you back, Pooky. I hope you've had a relaxing weekend break."

"Indeed I have, Miss!" said Pooky.

Mrs Paige picked up her chalk and wrote on the black board. "Now, today we are going to talk about the beginning of the time of the Stone Age!" she announced. "So, can anyone tell me what species of humans there are?" she asked.

"Some humans are Homo Sapiens, and some are the Neanderthals!" called out Pooky.

"Yes, very good Pooky!" replied Mrs Paige. "You see, Homo Sapiens and Neanderthals are several types of humans." Then she added, "They didn't have brick houses or working factories in those days, and they had to hunt animals to kill and eat, such as mammoths and boars amongst others."

It was really fascinating. All the children in the class were very amused by it, especially Pooky.

Meanwhile, at the Poo Factory, Percy the parrot was very tired from carrying the heavy bucket from the toilet and taking it to the machine to make more horrible and disgusting food.

Just then, the wizard and the witch came in from the kitchen. "OK, you good for nothing parrot!" snapped the wizard. "You can go and fly around the area now."

"We are going out for the day!" the witch announced. "And when we get back, we want that cauldron filled with clean water right up to the brim! Do you understand?"

"Yes, I do!" replied Percy breathlessly. With that, the wizard and the witch walked out of the factory and away. Percy was glad that he could take a break from carrying the bucket of poo.

"I think I'll fly around London for half an hour," he said to himself, "then I can come back and fill the cauldron right up to the brim with clean water."

With that, Percy flapped his wings and took off into the sky and was soon flying around London. He felt glad to exercise his wings again.

Back at the school, the children were still studying about the Stone Age. Pooky and Amrita were talking quietly about how the Stone Age people made their own weapons and grew their own food.

Suddenly, Pooky felt her tummy rumbling and then, her bottom quietly farted.

Ppppppppffffffttttt!

"Oh no!" said Pooky.

Amrita knew that Pooky was desperate for the toilet, so she went to Mrs Paige and said, "Pooky needs the bathroom, Miss!"

"Right then, thank you for letting me know, Amrita," replied Mrs Paige. As she led Pooky out of the door, she said to the children, "I'm taking Pooky to the bathroom, so just carry on with your studying and I'll back in a minute." Then she and Pooky ran down the corridors. Up in the sky above the school, Percy was feeling a lot better now that he had exercised his wings.

"I think I'd better have a rest now, then I'll go straight back to the factory."

So, Percy flew down and perched on the edge of the open window of the toilets. While he was resting, he heard the bathroom door open. It was Mrs Paige bringing Pooky into the toilets. When they got there, Mrs Paige lifted Pooky's dress up while Pooky dealt with her tights and underwear, then she lifted the toilet lid and sat down very gently and quietly.

"Ah, that's better!" she said with a smile. "Thank you Miss, I'm sorry I had to drag you out of class again."

"Don't worry about it," said Mrs Paige. "I'm just going back to check on the children, I'll be back in twenty minutes."

"OK, Miss!" replied Pooky.

Mrs Paige closed the door half-way and went back to the class to see how the children were getting on.

Pooky was sat on the toilet wondering how she could make her life a lot better, when she looked out of the open window and saw a bright handsome parrot that she had never seen before.

"Hello!" called Pooky. "What a beautiful parrot you are!"

Percy heard Pooky talking to him, so he looked in and saw her sitting on the toilet smiling up at him. Percy spread out his wings, flew down in through the open window and perched gently on Pooky's arm.

"Hello there, what nice manners you have!" said Percy.

Pooky was surprised. "I've never met a talking parrot before!" she announced.

"Well, now you have," he said. "My name is Percy, and I am very pleased to meet you."

"My name is Pooky Beaumont, and I am pleased to meet you too," replied the little girl.

"Pooky? That's a funny name. Unless it's a special name," he said in puzzled way.

"Yes! You see, my parents called me Pooky because I'm a special little girl," she explained.

Just then, outside of the school, Hector and Rocky sneaked into the playground, making sure that they were not noticed by the teachers.

"We will soon teach that smelly girl a lesson!" whispered Hector.

"Indeed, we will!" said Rocky.

As they sneaked past under the open window, they thought they heard someone talking.

"Did you hear someone talking?" asked Rocky.

"I did my friend!" answered Hector. They looked around, but they couldn't see anyone, so they carefully peeped in through the open window and saw Pooky chatting to a talking parrot.

"How did she get that parrot?" Hector gasped.

"I don't know," replied Rocky. "Let's listen and see!" So, they pressed their ears against the wall and listened.

Chapter 17
Sharing Stories

Percy was enjoying himself, talking to Pooky. "Shall I tell you my life story, Percy?" asked Pooky.

"Oh, yes please!" replied Percy.

"Well, when I was four-years old, I began suffering from a runny tummy," began Pooky. "Now, when I am doing my homework or playing with my toys, I feel my tummy rumbling and then a little fart comes out of my bottom."

"That sounds painful!" Percy gasped.

"It is!" Pooky agreed. "And the children of this school are always making fun of me and being nasty to me. But the two most horrid bullies of all are Hector and Rocky."

"Did they always bully you?" Percy asked.

"Yes they did!" answered Pooky. "They always kept teasing me, picking on me and calling me rude names like Smelly Poo."

Percy felt sorry for her.

"They even played nasty tricks on me. Once they placed a bucket of poo on top of the classroom door and when I opened the door to go back into the lesson, the bucket tipped over and landed on me and I was covered in poo!"

"Oh, that's horrible!" cried Percy.

"Indeed!" said Pooky. "They even pushed my head down the toilet and I was covered from my head to my neck in filthy poo, and I didn't really like that at all!"

Pooky took a deep breath and went on. "But now, Miss Hurricane, the school headmistress, has expelled Hector and Rocky and I am glad that I'll never be bullied by those two naughty boys ever again!"

Percy scratched his head with his foot and smiled. "Well, at least I know now that you are a very special little girl indeed!" he said. "Now that I've heard your story, would you like to listen to mine?"

"Yes please, Percy!" replied Pooky.

So Percy cleared his throat and began to tell Pooky his story. "Many years ago, I was born in the jungle of Africa and lived with my lovely family. We would fly around the sky with the other parrots, and we would watch the sun go down every evening.

"Then, one day, a great massive storm came and destroyed everything in its path. The huge tree, which was the home of me and my family, was blown over by the strong wind and it crashed to the ground."

"Were you frightened, Percy?"

"Yes, I was frightened, because the storm killed not only my whole family but all the other parrots in our part of the jungle. Then just when I was wondering what to do, I was caught in a big net and struggling to get out. I saw that two people were holding the net and discovered that they were magical people, a wizard and an ugly witch."

Pooky shuddered with worry. "So, what happened next?"

"They looked at me, said what a brightly colourful parrot I was and added that I would make a fine jailbird. I didn't know what they were talking about, but I noticed a magic ball and soon realised that they were the ones who had made the massive storm that had killed my whole family."

Percy lowered his head and a tear trickled down his beak. Pooky felt sorry for him and gave him a hug.

"It's OK, Percy," said Pooky, "I know how you feel."

That made Percy a little bit better. "That was a nice hug, Pooky," he said, wiping away the tears with his wing. "After they captured me, I was placed in a cage, magically transported along with them to London and taken to an abandoned factory. It was horrible and very smelly too."

"Is that why you ended up working with them?" asked Pooky.

"Exactly!" replied Percy. "They trained me to speak and made me carry a heavy bucket of poo from the toilet to a special machine, where they used the poo and the rotten foods that they had to make fresh smelly food and sell it in the market."

Pooky thought about it for a moment, and she remembered what Mr Desai had said the night before, then she said, "So maybe that's why everyone is feeling ill after buying the rotten food from the market!"

Percy was surprised and said, "Do you think so?"

"I do, Percy," she said. "Do you think I should keep quiet about it?"

Percy thought for a minute and then, turning to Pooky he said, "Yes, I think it's best if you don't say anything, because those villains will stop us from telling the people about it!"

So Pooky agreed to keep quiet. "Well, it was very nice to meet you, Percy." She smiled. "And I hope we'll meet up again someday."

"I'm sure we will!" replied Percy. "And if I were you, I would stay away from the Poo Factory, because they are looking for someone to be a slave and work in that horrible place on the other side of London." He went on.

"Thanks for telling me that," said Pooky. "I would much rather stay safe and be with my family."

"Precisely!" agreed Percy. "And now I'd best be off. Goodbye Pooky, look after yourself!" he added, and with that he spread out his wings, flew out of the window and was off through the sky.

"Goodbye, Percy, take care!" cried Pooky. Neither of them realised that Hector and Rocky had heard everything.

"Now that we know about that parrot's story," Hector said with ghoulish grin on his face, "perhaps we can get rid of that smelly girl after all."

"I quite agree!" Rocky smirked. "Let's follow that parrot and see where he is heading!"

So, they sneaked out of the school playground, climbed onto their bicycles, and started to follow Percy.

Back in the bathroom, Pooky was just finishing on the toilet when Mrs Paige came back.

"Hello, Pooky, are you alright now?" she asked. Pooky remembered Percy's warning and didn't say anything.

"Yes, Miss, I'm alright now!" was her only reply.

So, Mrs Paige wiped and cleaned Pooky's bottom and Pooky pulled her drawers and tights back up, then she washed her hands and walked with Mrs Paige back to the classroom, still thinking about her new friend, Percy.

Chapter 18
The Discovery

Meanwhile, Hector and Rocky were on their bicycles following Percy to try and find out where he was flying to. They followed the parrot all around London, then they cycled across the Thames and through the streets.

Percy, flying through the sky, had no idea that Hector and Rocky were following him. At last, he flew back to the Poo Factory, went in through his window and rested on his perch. Outside, Hector and Rocky arrived at the gates and stopped when they felt the horrible smell.

"What a dreadful smell!" they spluttered, then they saw the parrot sitting on his perch and realised that there must be people inside.

"I wonder what kind of factory this is?" Hector snorted.

"Maybe there are some mysterious people in there!" suggested Rocky.

"You are absolutely correct!" said a voice. Hector and Rocky turned around and saw the wizard and witch, who were returning from their day out.

"Hello there, young lads!" said the witch. "Can we help you?"

Hector and Rocky paused for a moment, then Hector asked, "Do you know what kind of factory is this?"

The wizard smiled at him and replied, "That is the Poo Factory!"

"Did he say Poo Factory?" asked Rocky in a gasping way.

"Yes, he did!" said Hector.

The wizard and the witch climbed down from the cart and explained, "The factory that you are looking at was old and abandoned, so when we came here, we decided to use it as a place to live and work."

"We use poo and rotten food and put them into a very special machine that magically mixes everything into new smelly foods," explained the witch. "And when they're done, we disguise ourselves and sell the food in the market," she added.

"That sounds revolting!" said Hector.

"Incredibly horrible!" added Rocky.

Then Hector spoke to the wizard, "Are you looking for a way to make this factory a lot busier?"

"Well, now that you mention it, we're trying to find a slave to sit on the toilet and fill it right up to the brim with poo!" exclaimed the wizard.

Hector and Rocky looked at each other and grinned an evil smile.

"Well, we know someone who can be your slave forever!" they said.

The wizard and the witch became interested by this. "Oh, splendid!" they cried, as Hector explained.

"In the Victorian School, on the other side of London, there is this little girl called Pooky Beaumont. She keeps pooping on the toilet at all times of the day and me and Rocky always bully her."

"But now we're expelled, thanks to her, and we want to get our revenge by getting rid of her!" fumed Rocky.

"I see!" said the wizard. "So how do you know all of this?"

"Well," said Hector as he went on, "we overheard that parrot talking to her in the toilets at the school this morning and we secretly followed him to the factory."

The wizard and the witch looked at each other in surprise. "What? That good for nothing parrot was at your school?" the witch cried.

"Yes, and that's how we got the idea about her becoming your slave in that factory!"

The villains thought for a moment, then they looked at Hector and Rocky and said, "Do you know what? I think that is an excellent idea!" So they began to make a plan.

"Is there a basement in the school?" they asked. The boys said that yes, there was a basement.

"Then here's what we want you to do!" said the witch.

"All you've got to do is lure that girl into the basement and we'll hide behind the boxes. Then, when she comes in looking for something, we'll knock her unconscious!" The wizard snorted. "We will dress her in old peasant clothes, put her in a sack, load her onto our cart and bring her back here to the factory."

Then the witch said, "And in return, we'll give you a bowl of pigeon pie for you to eat every single Monday!"

Hector and Rocky adored the thought of pigeon pie. "You've got yourself a deal!" they declared.

"Excellent!" the wizard said with delight. "We will meet you outside the Victorian School tomorrow morning and put our plan into action," he added.

"You got it!" replied Hector.

"What will you do with the parrot?" asked Rocky.

"Oh. Don't worry about him. We'll take care of that!" The Witch sniggered, as they shook hands.

The boys waved goodbye and cycled for home discussing their plans to set a trap for Pooky the next day.

Chapter 19
Setting the Trap

The next morning, Pooky, Amrita, Donald and Douglas were at school as usual. The boys were in their classroom learning how to use numbers and the girls were in Mrs Paige's class studying more about history that happened long ago.

Outside the school, Hector and Rocky were sitting behind the wall, making sure that no one in the school saw them, waiting for the wizard and the witch to arrive.

"We'll soon have that wretched girl gone forever!" whispered Hector.

"Then we can eat pigeon pie whenever we want!" Rocky grinned.

Just then, from around the corner, a horse and cart came into view. In the cart were the wizard and the witch in their disguises. Soon, they pulled up alongside Hector and Rocky. "Morning boys! Have you thought how to get that girl into the basement?" asked the wizard.

"We have!" Rocky said as he scratched his hands. "We have written a note from Mrs Paige to Pooky asking her to go into the basement and get a skipping-rope."

"So, when the bell rings for break time and all the children are out in the playground, Pooky will see the note on the teacher's desk and then she will go into the basement. Only you two will be waiting to knock her out cold and take her away with you," Hector said in a thinking kind of way.

"Marvellous," the wizard said. "Now, if you pass the note to me, we'll turn invisible so no one will be able to spot us and sneak into the classroom!"

The boys handed the note to the wizard, then he and the witch magically turned themselves invisible and began to sneak into the school quietly.

They walked silently through the corridor looking for Mrs Paige's classroom. Soon, the witch pointed and whispered, "Psst! There's the girl!"

They looked in through the window and there was Pooky, sitting at her desk, studying her history work.

Suddenly, the school bell rang. It was break time. All the children began to put their pencils and books down on their desks.

Mrs Walden came in and said, "Excuse me, Mrs Paige, but Miss Hurricane wants to speak to you right away!"

"Tell her I'll be there in two minutes," said Mrs Paige. As the door was already open, the wizard sneaked into the room, placed the note that Hector and Rocky had written on her desk, then sneaked quietly out again.

"Everything's ready!" said the wizard. "Let's get to the basement and wait for her to come in!" So they set off for the basement.

Mrs Paige and the children began to walk out of the classroom to go and have their break. Pooky was just following behind when she saw the note on the desk. She walked over to it, picked it up and began to read.

The note on the paper said:

"Pooky,
I'm just going to see the headmistress so, while I'm in her office, I want you to go into the basement and find a skipping-rope to play with for the afternoon break.
From Mrs Paige."

That's funny! thought Pooky. *Mrs Paige never usually leaves a note for me to look at. Oh well, I'd better do what she says.*

With that, she put the note back on the desk, walked out of the classroom and went to the basement to find a skipping rope.

The wizard and the witch were behind some piles of boxes waiting to capture Pooky.

"Do you think it will work?" asked the witch curiously.

"Of course, it will work, you silly old hag!" snapped the wizard.

Then they heard the door open and saw Pooky coming into the room.

"There she is. Get ready!" the wizard whispered.

Pooky looked around the basement and saw a box full of school toys. She went over and rummaged through the box. She was so busy that the wizard could carefully sneak up behind her holding a school bat in his hands. Then, just as Pooky lifted her head up so she could see the inside of the box, the wizard hit Pooky on her head with the bat with a very big thwack!

Pooky fell backwards onto the floor and lay there unconscious.

"Perfect! I told you that our plan would work!" cried the wizard.

The witch looked at Pooky and felt a bit disappointed, but she didn't say anything.

"Let's get her out of these clothes and put on those peasant ones," instructed the wizard. They worked as quickly as they could changing her from her nice new dress to the rotten old clothes.

When they had finished dressing her in old poor peasant clothes, they put her in a big sack and became invisible again. Then they walked out of the basement, through the corridor and sneaked out of the school to their cart, where Hector and Rocky were waiting.

"We've got her!" announced the wizard. "Thanks to you we can make her do all the work to make more smelly food!"

Hector and Rocky felt very pleased with themselves, especially when the witch magically presented them with a bowl of pigeon pie.

"Here you are boys. We will send another dish of pigeon pie to you next Monday!" said the witch.

"Thank you!" said Hector.

"I'm glad our deal is done!" added Rocky as the boys waved goodbye and went home to eat the pie.

The wizard and the witch loaded the girl onto the back of the cart and then they set off back to the Poo Factory.

Chapter 20
The New Slave

Percy was taking a break from carrying that heavy bucket. He was sitting on top of the roof looking at the other side of London. "I just wish I could find a way to escape from this revolting place!" he said to himself.

Then he looked down and saw the wizard and the witch returning. "Uh oh! I'd better get back to work or they'll skin me!" cried Percy. Then he flapped his wings and flew right back into the factory.

The wizard and the witch drove their horse and cart through the gates and came to a stop outside the doors.

"Right, you ugly hag, help me get this girl into the prison cell!" ordered the wizard. The witch had some second thoughts, but she did as she was told.

They carried the sack, with Pooky inside it, up to the second floor and soon, they came to the prison cell. The wizard took out a key from his pocket and unlocked the door.

They took Pooky out of the sack and placed her on an old dirty bed. "Now all we have to do is wait until she wakes up and then we'll tell her that she is our slave!" said the wizard. Suddenly, the witch noticed Pooky slowly moving on the bed.

"I think she is starting to wake up," she whispered.

Pooky slowly woke to find herself in a room with brown walls, and it was rotten and smelly.

"Oh, my head!" Pooky groaned. "I wonder why I am in this prison cell."

She looked to one side and saw the wizard and the witch standing beside her.

"Hello Pooky," said the wizard, "I am honoured to meet you!"

"How do you know my name?" asked Pooky, looking puzzled.

"We have learned from the talking parrot that you have a runny tummy," explained the wizard.

The witch stepped forward, adding, "That's why you have been chosen to be our slave."

"A slave?" asked Pooky.

"Yes! You are exactly the kind of person we want to be our slave forever!" announced the wizard.

"How come I'm in this prison cell and why am I wearing this old dirty dress?" Pooky wondered.

"Because you are a very special little girl indeed!" replied the wizard.

Then Pooky asked, "What do you mean you have learned from a talking parrot?"

"Well, our parrot, Percy, was at your school talking to you and when he flew back here two peasant boys followed him and explained everything to me!" said the wizard. Then he brushed his jacket with his hands and demanded Pooky to get onto her feet. Pooky did as he asked.

"Now, if you would like to follow me and the witch, we'll show around the Poo Factory and the work you needed to do," he announced. Pooky followed them as they began to walk all around the factory.

They took her to the toilet and the wizard began to explain, "As our slave, you must keep on pooing and pooing right up to the brim and when you've done that, I want you to take those two buckets, go around to the back of the toilet and fill them up with poo."

Then they took her to the room where a big machine was working. "This is where you bring the poo, and you will pour it into that chute. We'll do the rest by making the rotten smelly food," explained the witch.

Pooky was suspicious. "So, how long must I do all this work for?" she asked.

"From six o'clock in the morning till nine o'clock at night!" said the wizard. "And you will stay in this factory forever and ever," he added.

Pooky was a bit frightened and slightly confused. "What would happen if I refuse to work?" she asked worriedly.

"Well, if you refuse, we kill you and put you into the machine," replied the wizard.

Poor Pooky didn't want to stay in that horrible poo factory, but she didn't want to be killed either, so she reluctantly agreed to become their slave forever.

"Good girl!" The wizard smiled. "Now, if you follow us to our study, we'll give something to make your tummy runnier!"

Then they headed off to the wizard and the witch's study.

Chapter 21
The Crime Scene

Meanwhile, back at the Victorian School, everyone was in their classrooms doing their studies. Mrs Paige was writing on the black board about people in the Middle Ages. Then she turned and spoke to the children.

"Now class, I want you to write about anything that happened in the Middle Ages and then we can..." Just then she stopped and looked down. There she noticed the note that the naughty boys had written.

"That's funny," she said. "I don't remember writing that for Pooky." She looked up and saw that Pooky wasn't at her desk. She looked at the note and noticed the word 'basement', so she called Amrita over. "Would you go to the basement and see if Pooky is there please?" she asked.

"Of course, Miss!" replied Amrita, and she set off to the basement to find her best friend. Soon, she arrived and went inside to take a look. "Hello? Pooky? Are you in here?" she called, but no one answered, so she looked around the basement and searched behind the boxes then, just as she was about to go to the other side of the basement, Amrita looked down and saw Pooky's clothes on the floor. "What are Pooky's clothes doing on the floor?" said Amrita, then she looked to one side and saw the school bat. She examined it closely and saw, on the end of the bat, a large spot of blood and a bit of hair.

"Oh, my goodness!" she cried. "Pooky has been mu…mu…murdered!" and ran out of the basement screaming wildly. "Aaaggghhh!" Mrs Paige heard her and ran to see what was wrong.

"Amrita? What is it? What's wrong?"

"Oh, Miss," sobbed Amrita as she was in tears. "I've found all her clothes on the floor in the basement, then I saw that the school bat had some blood and a bit of hair on it. I think she's been murdered!"

"Oh no!" cried Mrs Paige as she took Amrita by her hand and went to tell Miss Hurricane what had happened.

In the headmistress' office, Amrita explained how she'd found Pooky's clothes, and the bat covered in blood and hair. "It was a really horrible sight. I was shocked when I saw it," she said with a shiver.

"Well, you did the right thing to tell us about it," said Miss Hurricane. "I'll phone the police immediately."

She turned to Mrs Walden and asked her to put her through to the police station. "Right away, Miss!" said Mrs Walden and rang the police as quickly as she could.

Police Sergeant Arnold Nesbit was in his office enjoying a cup of tea when the telephone rang. "Hello! This is Police Sergeant Arnold Nesbit speaking," he announced.

"Hello. It's Mrs Walden from the Victorian School," she said. "The headmistress wants to speak to you." Then she handed the phone over to Miss Hurricane.

"Thank you, Mrs Walden!" she said and began to speak.

"Hello Arnold, it's Miss Hurricane here."

"Hello Miss Hurricane! Have those two boys been causing trouble again?" he asked.

"No, I had them expelled!" she replied. "Anyway, we have another problem. Pooky Beaumont has disappeared, and it looks as if she has been murdered."

"Oh, that's terrible!" cried Arnold. "Was anyone with her before she disappeared?"

"Not really, but Amrita Desai was in the basement looking for her when she found the clothes and the bat," said Miss Hurricane.

"Right!" replied Arnold, as he finished his tea. "We'll be there right away!" he added.

A few minutes later, Police Sergeant Arnold Nesbit and his team arrived at the school to sort out the mess.

"Hello, Miss! We're here to put Pooky Beaumont's clothes and the school bat into separate bags," explained Arnold. Then he added, "We'll have to send all the children home until we've sorted out the crime scene."

"Very good, Arnold!" said Miss Hurricane. "I'll let the children know right away. Should we tell Mr and Mrs Beaumont about this?" she asked.

"Yes, I think we should!" said Arnold. "Me and my companion will go over and tell them what has happened," he added. Then he ordered his men to get to work on gathering up the evidence and to search for clues.

Chapter 22
The Very Sad News

Sergeant Arnold Nesbit and the police were busy in the basement sorting Pooky's clothes and the school bat into two bags. Then they looked around for any clues and noticed a bit of hair stuck on the front of the school bat.

"What do you think of this, Sarge?" asked one of the policemen. Arnold examined the hair carefully.

"Well, I think that bit of hair belongs to Pooky!" he said. "Take it to the lab and we'll see if it is," he added.

"Will do, sir!" said the policeman.

When they finished in the basement Arnold went to Miss Hurricane's office to report.

"What have you found?" she asked.

"Well, we have found all of Pooky's clothes and we noticed a bit of hair and some blood," explained Arnold.

"Was it Pooky's hair?" asked Miss Hurricane.

"We're just going to take it back to the lab to see if it is!" answered Arnold. "Did you send all the children home?" he asked.

"I did as you said," Miss Hurricane told him.

"Splendid! Thank you for letting us operate in the basement, Miss. I'll go around to the Beaumonts' house straight away and tell them about the crime scene," said Arnold.

"You're most welcome!" replied Miss Hurricane.

Arnold waved goodbye, climbed onto the police cart, and set off to see Mr and Mrs Beaumont.

At the house, Donald and Douglas were at home telling their parents about their day's work and about how everyone, including the twins, had been sent home early because of the crime scene.

"What crime scene?" asked Jack.

"We don't know," said Donald.

"We're waiting to see if someone really has been murdered," added Douglas.

Just then, there was a knock on the door. Igor went to the door, opened it, and there stood Police Sergeant Arnold Nesbit and his companion on the doorstep.

"Hello Officers!" said Igor.

"Hello Igor. Are Mr and Mrs Beaumont here?" asked Arnold.

"They certainly are! They are in the living room," announced Igor. "If you would like to follow me, I'll take you to them."

"Cheers!" Arnold replied, and Igor led them in. Igor opened the door of the living room and spoke to Jack and Penelope.

"Pardon me, Sir and Madam, but Police Sergeant Arnold Nesbit and his friend are here to speak to you."

"Thank you, Igor, send them right in," said Jack.

Igor bowed his head and then turned to the police and said, "You may go in."

They thanked Igor and walked into the living room. "Hello Jack, hello Penelope!" called Arnold.

"Hello there, Arnold, is there anything wrong?" asked Penelope.

"Well, I think it's best if we sit down because I'm afraid I've got some sad news," Arnold replied.

So, they all sat down on the sofas and on the chairs. "Jack and Penelope," began Arnold, "I am so sorry but there is no easy way to say this…your daughter, Pooky, well…we think she's been murdered!"

Donald and Douglas were shocked by this, and Jack and Penelope were horrified.

"What? Murdered?" cried Jack.

"Yes, I'm afraid so." Arnold sighed.

The twins hugged each other as tears rolled down their cheeks. "Why was she murdered?" they asked.

"Well, Amrita was in the basement looking for her and she found Pooky's clothes on the floor and the school bat with blood on it along with a bit of hair," explained Arnold.

Penelope was so shocked by the news she began to cry too.

"There, there, dear, it's alright," said Jack and gave her a big hug.

"I can't believe our beautiful girl has been murdered!" sobbed Penelope as she carried on crying.

"We think that someone out in London killed her," said Richard, who was a good friend of Arnold Nesbit.

"You're sure about this?" Jack asked as he hugged his wife.

"We're absolutely sure!" replied Arnold, and then he stood up and added, "We'll leave you to grieve over this sad news and I'll make sure that we find and capture the person who's responsible."

"Well, thank you for coming to tell us the sad news, Arnold," said Jack. "We'll try and cope with it somehow."

"It's our pleasure!" replied the police. They said their goodbyes, walked out of the living room and out of the front door.

"See you soon, Igor," called Arnold, and they went off back to the police station. Igor waved goodbye to them and quietly closed the door. He felt very sorry for the Beaumont family and wished there was something he could do to help. Igor went back into the living room and did his best to be cheerful.

"Are you OK, M'lady?" he asked kindly.

"I'm fine. I'm just upset because our poor girl is dead and now I'll never get the chance to say how much I love her, and she'll never see our new-born baby!" said Penelope as she dried her eyes from her tears.

"Don't worry, I'm sure everything will be alright in the end," replied Igor. "You wait and see!"

Chapter 23
Pooky's Terrible Work

Back at the poo factory, the wizard and the witch led Pooky to their magic room where they had lots of magic books, bottles, potions, and jars stacked on shelves and in the middle of the room was the magic ball which the wizard and the witch used.

"This is the room where we keep our books of spells amongst other things," said the wizard. "Now, if you wait over there, we'll show you our magic," he added.

Pooky did as the wizard asked. The wizard and the witch got to work to make a potion for Pooky. They mixed up cat whiskers, old mushrooms, honey, and rotten elderberries. When everything was mixed in, the wizard and the witch waved their hands over the cauldron and said the magic words which sounded something like this;

"Wacksy-backsy,
Wartkataffemall,
Turn this mixture
Into a candy ball!"

Then there was a flash of lightning and, from out of the cauldron, the wizard presented a small candy ball. The witch was worried and asked, "Are you sure that this candy ball is going to make that poor girl poo on the toilet?"

"Of course I'm sure you dumb-buffoon!" snapped the wizard angrily. "After all, we need to make lots more rotten food to sell," he added. Then he went over to Pooky and gave it to her.

"Here is a candy ball," said the wizard. "All you have to do is put it in your mouth, chew and swallow it down. When it's in your tummy, you will hear lots of rumbling and then you'll fart loudly and when that happens, you'll be sitting on the toilet," he added.

"When the toilet is full to the brim, you will go around to the back with the two buckets, fill them and bring them to the machine. Do you understand what I'm saying?"

"Yes, sir," replied Pooky quietly.

"Good girl!" the wizard said. "Now, let's take you back to your prison cell and you can wait until you feel your tummy rumbling and then you can start work right away!"

He turned to the witch and said, "Take her back to her prison cell, then return to me when you've done with her!"

The witch didn't like being told what to do, but quickly took Pooky back to the prison cell. Pooky popped the candy ball into her mouth and swallowed it down slowly.

As they walked, the witch kindly said, "Sorry about this, Pooky. I think you are the prettiest girl that I've ever met."

This made Pooky feel a little better. When they arrived at the cell, the witch opened the door and sat down with Pooky on her bed. "Were you always ugly like this?" asked Pooky. "I don't mean to be rude, but I just wondered if you had a nice face when you were little!"

The witch smiled a little smile and then she spoke, "Yes! When I was little, I did have a very pretty face. I was so pretty that my sister always thought that I was the loveliest girl in the world." The witch went on. "But when I was sixteen years old, an evil wizard appeared from nowhere and cast a spell on me, making me into an ugly witch and he brought me to work with him in this Poo Factory many years ago. I lost my family and have been stuck in this horrible place for a very long time!"

Pooky felt sorry for the witch and gave her a hug and, for the first time in her life, the witch felt loved again. She put her arms around Pooky and smiled.

"Don't you worry," said Pooky, "I'm sure you're still pretty too!"

The witch grinned and said, "I'm touched by your kind words and by the way, my name is Tiffany."

"Cool!" replied Pooky. "That's a nice name!" Suddenly, Pooky felt her tummy rumbling and then, there was a very loud noise.

Pppppppppppppppppppppppppppppffffffffffffffffffffffffffttttttttttttttttttt!

"Oh no!" cried Pooky, as she crossed her legs. "I think it's starting!"

Tiffany knew that Pooky was right, it really was starting. Luckily, there was a toilet on the other side of the cell. Pooky quickly ran and got there just in time. She lifted her dirty dress and sat down with a sigh of relief. "Phew, that was close!" she spluttered.

Tiffany stood up and said, "Well, at least you can relax now."

Then she said, "I'd better get back to the magic room before the wizard gets mad. I'll be back as soon as I can." And with that, she walked out of the prison cell and set off back to the magic room.

One hour later, Pooky had filled the toilet right up to the brim. She was very tired, but she knew that she had to carry on. So, she stood up and wiped her bottom with old tissue papers. When she had finished, she picked up the buckets and went around to the back of the toilet and began to shovel the poo into the buckets. It was smelly and dirty work.

Percy happened to be resting on the windowsill above the back of the toilet, when he looked down and saw a girl shovelling poo into the buckets.

She looks familiar, thought Percy. *I'm sure I've seen her somewhere before.* So he flew down to take a closer look.

Pooky was still shovelling when Percy landed on her arm and inspected her carefully. She looked up and saw the parrot.

Percy gasped and said, "Pooky, is that really you?"

Pooky, who almost didn't recognise Percy, also gasped. "Why hello Percy. Yes, it really is me."

"What are you doing here in the factory anyway?" Percy asked.

"I don't know, but I think I was lured into the school basement by someone who wants to get rid of me!" said Pooky.

Percy was shocked by this. "Who would do something like that?" he asked.

"I just wish I knew!" Pooky sighed.

Soon, she had filled the two buckets again, carried them to the machine, emptied them into it and then she went back to the toilet to shovel more. It was horribly hard work and Pooky was getting tired from going backwards and forwards. Now Pooky knew what it was like working in a disgusting smelly factory. She and Percy were trapped. They needed to think of some way to escape and fast.

Chapter 24
Pooky Cleans Up

A few days later, Pooky and Percy were working terribly hard. They carried bucket after bucket after bucket from the toilet to the machine. It was horribly complicated hard work and they got really dirty from the all the shovelling.

They started at six o'clock in the morning, worked throughout the day and into the evening up until nine o'clock at night. Pooky and Percy were getting very tired and tried to think of ways to escape, but they both knew that the wizard and the witch would do everything they could to stop them.

One day the wizard and the witch were in their study trying to think up new ideas of making horribly smelly food.

"What about revolting broccoli?" cried the witch.

"No, we've already done that!" The wizard sighed.

"Then we'll try and make some stinky cheese. Oh, we've already done that as well," replied the witch.

"Yeah! Quite right!" agreed the wizard. Then there was trouble. The wizard had just placed his hand onto a stack of books when he accidentally pushed them off the table along with two glass bottles. They fell to the floor with a crash! Everything was in a terrible mess.

"Oh fiddlesticks, look what I've done!" snapped the wizard, and called out from the doorway, "Pooky! Can you come in the magic study and clean up this mess for us?"

Pooky did as she was told and came in with a bucket of clean water and a mop.

"Now listen, I've accidentally knocked some of these books and two bottles off the table and they've crashed to the floor!" explained the wizard. "So, I want you to clean this up while me and the witch go out to the country to get some more elderberries from a farmer's bushes. Do you understand?"

"Yes, Sir!" said Pooky, nodding her head quietly.

"Splendid! We'll see you later in the afternoon," the wizard murmured. Then he and the witch left the room and set off to the countryside outside London.

After the wizard and the witch had gone, Pooky began to start sweeping up the mess that the wizard had accidentally caused. Ten minutes later, she had managed to clean up and scoop it into the bucket.

Just as she was about to leave the magic study, Pooky turned around and looked at the magic ball, which was placed on a pole.

Chapter 25
Pooky's Wish

Pooky walked over to the magic ball and took a closer look at it. "I wonder if it really can do magic," she said to herself, then she froze for a moment as Percy came flying into the room and landed on the magic table.

"Are you alright Pooky?" he asked.

"Yes, I'm OK! I was just looking at the magic ball," replied Pooky.

Then she looked at Percy and asked, "Are you sure this ball is really magic?"

Percy thought for a moment and answered, "I believe so!"

Pooky turned back to the magic ball and wondered if she could make a wish. So she put the broom and the bucket down, then walked over to the ball and paused for a second. After standing still for a while, Pooky placed her hands on the magic ball, closed her eyes and wondered what to wish for. Percy was a little worried about her putting her hands on the ball.

Finally, Pooky opened her eyes and began to make a wish. "I wish that I had special good magic powers to help the world!" she said. Suddenly, there was a rumble, then all the bottles and jars on the shelves started to rattle and shake, and then the magic ball started to glow. Sparkles of stars and lights began whirling around Pooky and all of a sudden there was a great big, gigantic ginormous flash! Then everything became silent and still.

Pooky took her hands of the ball and gasped in shock. "Oh, my goodness, that ball really was magic!" cried Pooky.

"You can say that again!" agreed Percy, who was even more shocked than she was.

Pooky glanced around and looked at the broom that she had left with the bucket.

"I wonder if I could make that broom come to life?" she asked herself. So, she walked over and waved her hands over the broom and said some magic words that went something like, *"Abracadabra, good and strife, make this broom come to life!"*

Instantly, her hands glowed, and sparks flew around the broom. There was another flash, and, to Pooky's surprise, the broom did come to life. It had grown arms, hands and gained a handsome face. The broom yawned and looked around the room. Pooky, who was watching from the middle of the room, was delighted.

"I did it! I did it! I really can do magic!" she shouted and, for the first time in months, Pooky danced around the table with joy and laughter.

After about five minutes of celebrating her wish, she went over to the broom and said, "Hello, my name is Pooky Beaumont, and I am your master!"

The broom politely bowed and smiled, "Hello, Ma'am, I am honoured to serve you and what is your command?"

Pooky thought for a minute and scratched her head, then she had an idea.

"Well, you can call me Sorceress and I would like you to carry that bucket of broken bits of glass to the rubbish bins and tip it all in please!" She began. "And I will call you Broomstick Billy," she added.

"Hmm, I like that name. It's perfect!" he said, "I'll get started right away."

So, Billy picked up the bucket and began to take it to the rubbish bins. Pooky smiled as she watched her creation doing the work, then she turned to Percy.

"Well Percy, I think we're going get out of here when the time comes," said Pooky.

"Indeed, that was totally wicked!" squawked Percy with glee. Then, he flew over to Pooky's shoulder and they walked out of the magic room.

Chapter 26
The Secret Is Now Revealed

Now that Pooky, Percy and Broomstick Billy are working happily together the job is much quicker. While Pooky sat on the toilet and filled it up with poo, Billy would shovel the poo into the buckets and carry them to the machine. He was so very fast and quick that the job was soon done.

At last, they finished their work and sat down in the prison cell for a rest.

"You were great Billy and you've managed to fill the cauldron right up to the brim!" said Pooky.

"Thank you, Sorceress!" replied Billy. "I am glad that you brought me to life so that I can do anything for you."

"Precisely!" She nodded. Just then Percy looked out of the window and saw the wizard and the witch coming through the gates.

"Quick! They're back!" he cried.

Pooky turned to Billy and said, "Now then Billy, you must blend in as a normal broom when they're around, they must never know that I've brought you to life! Do you understand what I'm saying?"

"Absolutely!" said Billy and went stood in a corner of the room to blend in just as Pooky asked.

Pooky and Percy began to walk to the front door to greet them. But just as Pooky was about to open the doors, she heard voices outside. *I wonder what's going on?* she pondered, opened the door just a tiny bit and peeped out.

There she saw the wizard and the witch talking to Hector and Rocky by the horse and cart.

"What on earth are those two naughty boys doing here?" she asked Percy.

"I don't know." He sighed. "We'd better listen and see what they are talking about."

They carefully made sure that they were not seen and listened to the conversation. "Great to see you again boys!" greeted the wizard and he magically gave them another bowl of pigeon pie.

"Thanks!" said Hector.

"I simply don't know how you do it, but it looks good!" replied Rocky.

The wizard smiled and said, "It surely does, and you deserve it after you managed to get your revenge by tricking that girl into the basement, knocking her unconscious and giving her to us as a slave to work in our factory."

Pooky and Percy, who had been hiding under an old cart, were shocked by their discussion and Pooky realised that it was Hector and Rocky who had been trying to get rid of her. She put her hand to her ear and carried on listening to what they were saying.

"I am glad that she is working so hard. I think we will have to move up to the next level," declared the wizard.

"What do you mean move up to the next level?" asked Tiffany.

"Well," explained the wizard, "I think we'll move up by killing her and throwing her into the machine along with all the rotten food and poo."

Tiffany was horrified. "You don't mean to sacrifice that poor innocent girl by turning her into rotten food, do you?" she said.

"Absolutely!" said the wizard. "We are going to kill the girl by stabbing her in the heart four times and then we'll drop her into the machine, mix her and everything else together and magically change them into more rotten food!"

"Ooh! That will be even better!" cried Hector. "And it will be even more fun!" added Rocky. Tiffany didn't know what to do or say. She had thought that being an evil witch would be fun, but she knew that killing a little girl was too much and she soon realised it wasn't fun after all.

"Look, I know that we're making excellent progress, but have you actually thought this through?" she asked.

The wizard walked over and seized her hair with his hand. "Of course, I have thought this through, you stupid witch! Once she has filled up the cauldron with poo, we will be ready with sharp knifes to kill her and you boys can help me."

Hector and Rocky were delighted. "We would be glad to help you, and no one will never find out about this whole thing," they said.

"Fantastic!" The wizard grinned, then he looked at his watch. "Well, we'd better go inside and make our plans for tomorrow."

Pooky and Percy were so shocked by their plans that they carefully sneaked back into the factory. Once they were in, Pooky ran as quickly as she could, with Percy still perching on her shoulder, back to the prison cell.

They reached the cell just in time. Pooky laid down on the bed pretending to be exhausted by the day's work and Percy sat on his perch and pretended to be asleep. A moment later, the wizard came into the cell with Tiffany following behind.

"Ah, Pooky, thank you for cleaning up the mess in the magic room," he said. "Now, I want you to carry on filling the toilet with poo and taking it to the machine as usual tomorrow and, when you have finished the job, wait in the cell and I will come in with a little surprise for you." He went on.

"I'm very grateful!" said Pooky quietly.

"I know!" replied the wizard, hiding his evil scheme, knowing that tomorrow would be the day to murder Pooky. "Now get a good night's rest and I'll see you in the morning!"

Then he turned to go out the door. "Are you coming?" he asked the witch.

"I'll be right with you, I just need to have a few moments with the girl," replied Tiffany.

"Suit yourself," said the wizard and went off back to the study to do his magic.

Chapter 27
The Meeting

After the wizard left the prison cell, Tiffany sat down on the bed next to Pooky and spoke to her, "Are you feeling OK?"

"Well, I cleaned up the mess and completed the job, but now I am going to be murdered and be turned into rotten food!" said Pooky as she shivered in fright.

Tiffany gasped and said, "Did you overhear the plans?"

"Yes, and I've found out that it was those two naughty boys who were responsible for tricking me into the school basement and knocking me out cold."

Percy was more worried than ever, and he wondered aloud, "How are we going to get out of here if they are going to kill you?"

Pooky thought for a moment, then an idea came into her head. "I've got it!" she cried and turned to Tiffany. "You have been an ugly witch for all your life, and you have never had the chance to be lovely," she said. "Well, I think I might be able to solve your problem." Then she instructed Tiffany to stand in the middle of the room.

"Now stay still," Pooky advised and then began to cast a magic spell by saying, *"Abracadabra, Jollibeanibull, Make this poor woman very beautiful!"*

Suddenly there was a flash and a puff of pink fluffy smoke. When the smoke cleared, Pooky looked at Tiffany, then she smiled.

"Wow Tiffany, you look beautiful!" said Pooky, then she cast a mirror. *"Let there be a mirror on the wall!"* she chanted and there, on the wall, was a mirror. "Have a look at yourself," declared Pooky.

Tiffany looked. She gasped and, for the first time in a long while, her ugly face was gone. It had been replaced by a very pretty face with lovely orange-ginger hair. "Golly!" said Tiffany, "I look so…so…"

"…Wonderful?" finished Percy politely as he admired her gorgeous new looks.

"Yes, and cute too!" she added.

Tiffany walked over to Pooky, got down on her knees and gave her a big kiss on the cheek.

"Thank you Pooky, you have changed me back to my original beauty!" she said as a tear rolled down from her eyes.

"That's alright," said Pooky. "It is nice to see good witches having a great body and a lovely face."

"I quite agree!" cried Percy. "Now, what are we going to do?"

Everyone thought for a while and then Pooky said, "I think I might have the answer."

She put two fingers in her mouth, whistled like a bird and Billy came into the cell as quick as a hare. Tiffany was surprised to see a live broom in the room.

"Tiffany, this is Broomstick Billy and Broomstick Billy, this is Tiffany," exclaimed Pooky.

"Nice to meet you, Tiffany!" said Billy. "Did you want me for something, Sorceress?" he asked.

"Yes, I did! Now, I have got an idea how we can teach that horrible wizard a lesson," began Pooky. "Tomorrow he is going to kill me and throw me into the machine after I have filled the toilet as usual." Then she stopped.

"What is it Pooky?" they asked.

"Well, I've just thought of something," she answered. "I wonder if my magic powers can cure my tummy problem."

She closed her eyes, took a deep breath, and began chanting, *"Abracaposes, Musabunear, Make the diarrhoea in my tummy disappear!"*

At once, sparkles of stars and the magic from Pooky's hands danced around and finished with a puff of pink smoke. When all the smoke had cleared, Pooky looked down at her tummy, then she stood very still and waited for something to happen. But it didn't.

Everyone stared at her for a moment and Tiffany asked, "Did you feel a little fart?"

Pooky looked at her and replied, "No, it's gone! It's really gone!"

Pooky was so delighted that she danced up and down the cell crying, "Hooray, I'm cured!" Everyone was thrilled and delighted that Pooky's tummy trouble was over.

"Now," said Pooky as she finished dancing around the room, "gather around and I'll tell you my idea how to give the wizard and the boys a taste of their own medicine."

Chapter 28
The Confused Wizard

They all sat down on the floor of the cell and Pooky explained about her plan, "We already know that the wizard is going to kill me tomorrow after I've completed the job, right?" Everyone nodded in agreement. "Well, I think we should play tricks on him by making him think that there are a lot of working brooms in the factory."

Then she turned to Billy and said, "I'm going to make a lot more magic brooms, so you won't have to be the only one." Before Billy could answer Pooky stood up and began to do her magic.

She wiggled her hands and said, *"Once this magic broom is working, what was one should now be twenty!"* she chanted and suddenly, nineteen brooms appeared around Billy, and they all looked exactly like him.

They all said, "Hello Broomstick Billy!" and bowed at Pooky.

Billy was delighted and said, "That is great. Now I have got some friends to work with, but how's that going to help?"

"Well, I believe that each broom should take turns to play tricks on Hector, Rocky and the wizard," explained Pooky, "and you are the leader of the brooms Billy."

"Gosh! I always wanted be a leader!" Billy smiled.

"Indeed, and I will pretend to sit on the toilet and fill it to the brim with poo, only I'll be using my magic powers to do it," she said. Then she turned to Tiffany. "I think you'd better find somewhere to hide before we can defeat him."

Tiffany agreed, and Percy said that he'd be keeping an eye on the wizard and the boys to make sure that they never got the chance to kill her.

The next day, Pooky gave the brooms their instructions and told them to hide around the factory. "Now, after you've filled the machine up with poo, we can make all sorts of frightening noises to scare them off," she explained.

"Of course, Sorceress, but what if that fails?" asked Billy.

"Then we shall have to work together to defeat him," she added.

Just then, Percy came in through the door and cried, "Quick, the wizard and the boys are coming!"

Billy ordered the brooms to hide, and they found lots of places inside the factory. Then Pooky, Percy and Billy hurried back to the prison cell and began to act naturally.

Billy went into a corner to blend in until Percy gave him the signal. Soon the wizard came into the room.

"Morning Pooky, I see that you've already filled the machine with poo and rotten food," he remarked.

"Indeed, Sir, just doing my job," said Pooky, as another idea came into her head. "What are you going to do now?" she asked.

The wizard was surprised and said, "What do you mean what am I going to do now? I always know what I am going to do because I always know everything."

Pooky smiled and replied, "Precisely. You, along with those naughty boys, Hector and Rocky, are going to kill me today."

This made the wizard confused. "I really don't know what you're talking about," he said in an angry way.

"Oh, but I think you do," answered Pooky and added, "because you wanted me to work in the poo factory forever, so you paid Hector and Rocky to trick me into thinking that Mrs Paige wanted me to go into the basement to fetch

something. They knocked me unconscious and then you changed me out of my clothes into old and dirty slave working clothes."

"That is not true!" protested the wizard.

"Oh yes, it is!" Pooky went on. "And then you loaded me onto the back of your cart and took me all the way to the poo factory. I know because I overheard you talking to them yesterday and, by the way, Tiffany has been kind to me ever since I worked here."

The wizard was shocked and said, "Do you mean the ugly witch who works alongside me?"

"Yes!" answered a voice from behind him. The wizard turned around and saw that it was Tiffany who was talking.

"What has happened to your ugly face and your oversized body?" asked the wizard. "You look different."

He stopped and thought for a moment, then he turned back to Pooky and looked at her. Suddenly, the wizard put two and two together and realised that it was Pooky who had changed Tiffany's life.

The wizard was absolutely furious, and his face turned red like a devil's. "You've changed that ugly old witch into a nice, beautiful woman!" he said angrily. "I'll get my revenge by killing you and turning you into rotten food!" he bellowed.

"Oh, I don't think so," exclaimed Pooky as she winked at Percy.

Percy flapped his wings and shouted, "Now!" Suddenly, Billy jumped out from the corner and gave the wizard a mighty whack!

"Ouch!" he cried and saw that a broomstick had just come to life. He soon realised that Pooky must have magic powers as well.

"You've taken my magic powers, you wicked little girl!" shouted the wizard furiously. "You are dead!" he added and ran to grab Pooky. But Tiffany picked up a bucket and threw it towards the wizard.

It hit him and he fell over backwards, landing on the floor with a splat!

"Run, Pooky, run!" shouted Tiffany.

Pooky jumped over the wizard and ran out of the cell. The wizard quickly stood up and angrily ran after her.

"Quick Billy. Get the other brooms to attack!" shouted Percy as he flew off to help stop the wizard.

"I'm on my way!" called out Billy. He placed two fingers in his mouth and whistled as loudly as he could.

Chapter 29
The Magical Battle

The nineteen brooms heard Billy's whistle and ran up to him as fast as they could. Meanwhile, Pooky ran all around the factory with the wizard angrily chasing her. Then Pooky saw a pile of boxes by the stairs, so she magically lifted them and placed them into a wall blocking the wizard's way and then she ran up the stairs right to the top.

The wizard crashed into the boxes and rolled over on the floor. He got up again and was just about to start chasing Pooky again when he heard a strange noise.

It seemed to be coming from the top of the stairs. The wizard thought it was Pooky up there, so he started to walk up to find her, unaware that she was hiding in one of the boxes.

"You can run but you can't hide!" cried out the wizard.

While he was climbing the stairs, Pooky got out of the box and began to do a magic spell, *"Make me invisible!"* she chanted and soon, she was invisible. Then she saw Hector and Rocky with very sharp knives. They were planning to stab her and kill her off.

"Smelly Poo will be dead as soon as we find her!" said Hector.

Rocky turned his head around and gasped as he tapped Hector on the shoulder.

"What is it?" he asked.

"Well look behind you!" Rocky trembled. Hector turned around and, to his shock and surprise there, behind the naughty boys, the magic brooms were all holding wooden swords and shields.

Billy raised his hand and shouted, "Attack!" The boys were so frightened that they started to run as fast as they could.

Tiffany, waving her magic wand, and Percy came running to join in the group.

Hector and Rocky ran, but then they said, "Why are we running? They're only a bunch of brooms!"

"Let's attack!" they cried and began to fight with the brooms.

Meanwhile, the wizard was still looking for Pooky when he heard sound of the fighting coming from downstairs. So, he hurried back down and saw the magic brooms and Tiffany attacking Hector and Rocky.

Close to the window, Percy was watching when he heard a quiet voice, "Psst, Percy, it's me! I'm here but I'm now invisible!" whispered Pooky.

"Are you OK?" asked Percy.

"Absolutely!" she replied. "Look, there's Police Sergeant Arnold Nesbit and his gang in the distance. I am going to magically light this barrel of gunpowder and throw it into the machine."

"But will it blow up?" Percy replied anxiously.

"Of course," she said. "Then we all need to run out of the factory as fast as we can before it explodes and that will attract the police." Percy pondered this for a moment, and, after some thought, he agreed gently.

Pooky and Percy began to pile up ten barrels of gunpowder and attach a long length of rope to one of the barrels.

As they prepared the barrels Pooky said, "Do you know when I said that the barrels are full of gunpowder?"

"Yes, why?" asked Percy.

"I've just magically turned the black gunpowder into a colourful powder."

"So, what you're saying is that the barrels will explode in colour?" replied Percy.

"Yes, that's right!" exclaimed Pooky.

Soon, they finished stacking the barrels and then hid behind some boxes. Downstairs, Tiffany, and the magic brooms were still battling against Hector and Rocky. The brooms were finding it difficult to fight, but they managed to dodge out of the way of the bullies.

"This is getting ridiculous!" snapped Hector.

"They're nothing but a bunch of stupid brooms!" added Rocky.

Suddenly, one of the brooms froze for a moment, then it got very angry and began to charge at them.

"Don't call me stupid!" the broom shouted. He swung himself and, with a huge 'whack', he knocked both Hector and Rocky to the floor. They both laid unconscious. Tiffany, Billy, and the brooms looked at them for a second.

"Good work lads!" congratulated Billy. "Now, you four take the boys outside and guard them while the rest of us go and stop the wizard," he added.

Chapter 30
The Colourful Explosion

The four brooms carried the two unconscious boys out of the factory, while the others set off to find Pooky and Percy. The wizard was still searching for the girl when he spotted some muddy footprints on the floor.

"Ah ha!" he said, grinning horribly. "Now I know where to find you." He tip-toed carefully and quietly, not wanting to make a noise in case Pooky knew. In the room where the barrels were to be exploded, Pooky and Percy were waiting to lure the wizard into their trap. "Percy, could you check to see if he's coming?" asked Pooky.

"But I don't want you to be killed after everything you've been through," protested Percy.

"I know Percy, I know. But I don't want you to worry, because the police will be here soon to arrest the wizard," smiled Pooky and she gave him a big hug. Percy felt a lot better after that and flew up onto a ledge to check.

After a minute or two he saw the wizard sneaking into the room. "He's coming Pooky!" he shouted, "Light the fuse now!"

Quickly, Pooky magically lit the fuse then ran and hid behind the door.

The wizard came into the room and began to search around. "I know you're hiding in here somewhere," he said in a tempting mood, "and then, when I'm done with you, I will take back your powers and have you cleaning and picking up poo for the rest of your life!"

He was so busy looking around the room that he didn't notice Pooky and Percy sneaking out and closing the door behind them. Nor did he hear the fuse getting closer and closer to the pile of barrels.

Outside, Pooky magically locked the door trapping the wizard inside and, after three steps back, she cried, "You're not gonna find me in there with ten barrels of gunpowder you big, dumb, bumbling sorcerer-ness!"

The wizard looked at the barrels and realised that they were about to blow up. He ran to open the door but found it was locked.

"Let me out this instant, you wicked little girl!" shouted the wizard angrily.

"Sorry, no chance!" Pooky denied.

"And you're going to get what you deserve!" added Percy.

Pooky, who quickly magically made herself visible again, started to run out of the factory as fast as she could with Percy following close behind her. As they ran, they saw Tiffany and the brooms looking for them. "Quick, get out of the factory as fast as you can!" shouted Pooky.

"It's going to blow!" cried Percy. After hearing the warning, they all ran out of the factory as quickly as they could.

Back inside the room, the wizard tried to open the door, but it was locked tight. He looked back at the barrels. The fuse was only ten inches away and it was getting closer. The wizard ran forward to try to stop them from blowing up, but it was too late. The barrels exploded with an almighty bang!

Pooky, Percy, Tiffany, Billy, and the rest of the magic brooms got out of the factory just in time and took cover as the Poo Factory began to explode. Not far away, Police Sergeant Arnold Nesbit and his team were walking along the High Street when he saw the factory blowing up.

"Golly-gosh!" he cried. "That factory's exploding like colourful fireworks! I think we'd better investigate immediately!"

So, they ran through the gates and into the yard to see what was happening. Suddenly, there was another very loud bang as one of the factory funnels exploded and, flying out of the factory, was the wizard.

He went shooting up into the sky like a rocket and then started to come straight back down. He flapped his arms as hard as he could, but he kept on falling down, down, down, to the ground.

"Heeelllpp!" cried the wizard, as he hit the ground with a giant wallop!

The wizard laid unconscious for a while and then slowly opened his eyes and gasped as he saw that he was surrounded by the police.

"Ello, Ello, Ello! What have we here?" pondered Sergeant Arnold.

"It looks like a nasty wizard who has been making rotten food out of poo!" replied one of the police constables.

"Exactly!" answered Arnold. Then he looked up and could not believe his eyes. There, right in front of him, was Pooky, all dressed in old clothes. She looked and felt a bit smelly, but she was smiling at him.

"Hello, Police Sergeant Arnold!" she called.

"Hello, Pooky," cried Arnold, as he went over to her. "Thank goodness you're alive! We all thought that you'd been murdered."

"Oh, I wasn't murdered. I was knocked out unconscious," said Pooky as she told him the whole story.

Arnold and the officers were amazed by her adventure, then she added, "I was being protected and cared for by a nice witch named Tiffany and a talking parrot named Percy." And sure enough, Percy and Tiffany came out from hiding holding onto the two boys.

"Well, I never!" exclaimed Arnold, "I never thought I'd see the day." He went up to Tiffany and said, "I don't know how to thank you for protecting this poor girl from danger, Ma'am."

"Oh, it was nothing," replied Tiffany. "I always wanted to be a good person inside and if it hadn't been for Pooky, I would still be the bad ugly witch."

"And I would be stuck in this disgusting Poo Factory forever," added Percy.

"I didn't know the parrot could speak English," said another police officer.

Tiffany began to tell Arnold about Hector and Rocky. "These two naughty boys, who used to be at the same school as Pooky, teamed up the wizard to get their revenge after the headmistress expelled them for being horrid to her. They left a fake note to make Pooky think that it was from Mrs Paige and then, when she went into the basement to find something, they knocked her out cold, took all her clothes off and dressed her in dirty old working clothes," she explained. "Then they loaded her onto the back of the cart and brought her back to the factory so the wizard could use her as a slave."

"That sounds very horrible and revolting!" agreed Arnold and turned to the boys. "You two are in really big trouble now! You shouldn't have tried to get your revenge by getting rid of Pooky. She is good-hearted, kind and the loveliest little girl and you should never have bullied, teased, or abused her! I'm going to have to arrest you both along with the wizard for your part in his evil plan," he added.

Hector, Rocky and the wizard were all handcuffed and dragged away to the police station. "I hope the judge will know what to do with them!" Arnold smiled.

"So do I!" said Pooky. "And I would like you to meet Broomstick Billy and the magic brooms." The police were amazed to see the brooms walking up to them and saluting politely.

"They're very good at that!" Arnold said. "I wish I could have an army of brooms in the force."

"Well, I think we'd be honoured to join the crew, Sir," said Billy. "We can also sweep up the streets and towns to make the world a better place to live, if Sorceress Pooky agrees." Pooky pondered for moment and then she smiled.

"Yes, of course I think you and the other brooms should go and work for the police force," said Pooky.

Billy and the brooms were grateful and thanked Pooky for everything she'd done for them.

"Right then," said Arnold, "we'd better take you to the hospital and get you checked over to see if you are injured." With that, he escorted Pooky, Percy and Tiffany to the carriage, then he asked one of his officers to go to the Beaumont house and tell everyone that they had found Pooky and were taking her to the hospital. The officer did as he was told and raced off as fast as he could. Arnold climbed into the carriage, and they set off for the hospital.

Chapter 31
A Happy Reunion

Soon, they arrived at the hospital and Dr Devonport was waiting outside when Police Sergeant Arnold Nesbit brought Pooky in. "Pooky is OK, but she just needs to be checked all over to see if there are any injuries," explained Arnold.

Dr Devonport understood what he said and called a nurse to bring a stretcher at once. They wheeled Pooky to the operating room and set to work checking her over from head to foot, while Arnold, Percy and Tiffany waited patiently in the waiting room for news.

Half an hour later, at half past three, the Beaumonts and Igor arrived after hearing from the police officer that Pooky had been found alive.

"Oh, Arnold!" cried Penelope. "How is she?"

"Well, Penelope, your daughter is fine. they're just checking her over," replied Arnold. "Allow me to introduce you all to Tiffany, the kind witch and Percy the Parrot," he added.

They were soon introduced and had the whole story explained to them. "We were very worried about Pooky," said Tiffany. "We knew that the wizard was going to kill her."

"But she managed to use her magic powers to stop him, and she was brilliant," replied Percy.

"She was a great friend too!" he added.

Just then, Dr Devonport came out of the operating room and spoke to them. "I am pleased to say that she is alright. She just has a bandage on her head and on her arm, but apart from that, she is fine." Then he added, "You can go in now, she will be very happy to see you."

The doctor led them through to the ward and opened the door. They walked up to Pooky's hospital bed and Penelope sat down on a chair beside her. She was fast asleep. They were delighted that she was safe and sound again and Penelope stroked her hair gently. A few minutes later Pooky slowly opened her eyes and sat up.

"Hello dear," said Penelope. Pooky turned her head and was so happy to see her family again that she jumped out of bed and gave her mum a warm hug.

"Hello, Mum," she said, as she hugged her. "I thought I would never see you again."

"Me too, sweetheart!" Penelope smiled, and gave her a kiss on her head.

"Your new friends, Percy and Tiffany, have told us the whole story about your adventure," said her father.

"It was really clever of you to defeat that nasty wizard!" cried Donald and Douglas. "Mr Desai will be pleased when he hears about how you've solved the mystery of the smelly food in the marketplace," they added.

"Oh, sweetheart, I am so proud of you," said Penelope, "and I think your new friends should come and live with us."

Pooky was delighted with this news and said, "I'd like that, Mum. Tiffany is good at cooking and keeping everything nice and tidy."

"Well then, Remy will be happy now that we've got two cooks, and Percy will be your pet and companion," announced Jack, and they all hugged together, especially Percy and Tiffany, who were glad that they were going to be part of the Beaumont family.

Chapter 32
Pooky's Welcome Home Party

A few days later, Pooky was feeling a lot better. She had a bandage on her right arm and some plasters on her head and hands, but her legs and feet were absolutely fine, and she could walk easily. She was ready to go home with her family. Pooky walked slowly towards the reception with her case to where her family were waiting.

Dr Devonport was there too and said, "Well, Pooky, I am glad you're much better. I'll come around in a few days to make sure that everything's alright again."

"Thanks for everything, Doctor!" said Pooky.

"See you soon."

Her parents wrapped their arms around her and walked out of the hospital to the horse and carriage. They climbed on board and set off for home. As they drove Penelope spoke, "You have had quite an adventure in that horrible Poo Factory."

"I certainly have!" she replied. "And I am glad that I have got marvellous magic powers and I'm happy now that the problem with my tummy has gone."

Jack smiled and spoke as he kissed her on her cheek, "Well, you are a very brave girl and there's a surprise for you when we get home." Pooky wondered what the surprise would be. Fifteen minutes later, they arrived, climbed out of the carriage, and walked up the steps to the front door. Penelope opened the door, and they went in. Pooky smiled as she was glad to be home.

Igor walked up and said, "Hello, Miss Pooky. We are glad to see you back home after that horrible wizard and those naughty boys gave you such a hard time."

"It's nice to see you too, Igor," said Pooky.

"Is everything alright?" asked Penelope.

"Oh yes, M'lady!" answered Igor. "If you would like to come with me, we'll go into the living room!"

They all walked to the living room door and then Igor said, "You go in first Miss Pooky and then we'll follow you."

Pooky opened the door and walked in, but it was dark. She switched on the light and suddenly, Donald, Douglas, Percy, Tiffany, the maids, Remy, the Desai family, Arnold Nesbit and the teachers all jumped out from behind the sofa and chairs and shouted, "Surprise! Welcome home, Pooky!" And they all cheered.

Pooky couldn't help but smile and laugh as she saw all her friends clapping and cheering. "Oh, what a wonderful surprise!" said Pooky, when she finished laughing. "Thank you so much everyone. They all sat down at the table and began to enjoy a delicious feast with drinks of lemonade and orange juice.

Donald and Douglas sat with Pooky between them, and they hugged each other with happiness. "We really had no idea that Hector and Rocky wanted their revenge on you after we saved you from them that day," they said.

"Oh it's not your fault, boys," said Pooky. "I am grateful for your protection."

"And I'm so glad that you're still alive," added Amrita, coming over to join them.

Mr Desai was having a good chat with Jack and Penelope about how Pooky had managed to solve the problem of the horrible foods in the market.

"I never thought that Pooky could solve the problem," said Mr Desai. "She really is a very special girl after all."

"You can say that again, Mr Desai!" agreed Jack as he drank a little of the lemonade from his glass.

Then Mr Desai added, "I shall give £100 pounds to your daughter as a thank you present, and she will be able to buy some nice dolls to play with."

"Thank you, Mr Desai. That's very kind of you," they said.

Amrita was admiring Percy as he told her about how the wizard killed his family, brought him to England to be his slave and how he'd met Pooky and helped her and Tiffany the witch escape from the Poo Factory.

"What an amazing story!" said Amrita, "I never thought you would be clever and brave enough to stand up to that horrible wizard."

Pooky looked at Percy and smiled as she spoke.

"Well, I think I have such a wonderful family and the most terrific friends in the world, and I've something for you."

Pooky took hold of Amrita's hand and said the magic words,

"Hocus Pocus, Friendship and cleverness,
Let there be a friendship necklace!"

Amrita couldn't believe her eyes. There in her hand was a beautiful necklace, with gold and silver beads on it.

"Oh, what a magnificent necklace," she said. "I didn't know you had magic powers," she added.

"Everyone's good at something when they find their courage," said Pooky, and Percy agreed. Later, when the party was over and it was time for everyone to go home, the Beaumonts thanked their friends for coming and wished them good night. They sat down on the sofas in the living room and the grown-ups had some tea and coffee to drink.

"What a party!" said Mitzi.

"It certainly was!" replied Sophie, as they cleared up the dishes and cups from the tables. Jack and Penelope looked at the children and grinned at each other.

"Our kids are starting to grow up," said Penelope.

"Especially Pooky," added Jack.

Penelope placed her hand on her tummy and rubbed it gently. "Soon they will have a new little brother or sister to play with," she said to herself.

Soon, it was bedtime, they all said goodnight to each other and climbed up the stairs to bed.

Chapter 33
A Happy Event

One week later, everything was all back to normal and Pooky, Percy, Donald and Douglas were in the playroom having fun. Pooky and Percy were playing a game of tea parties with the new dolls which Pooky had bought with the £100 Mr Desai had given her the day before, and Donald and Douglas were playing a game of cards. Just then there was ring at the door, and Igor went to answer it. It was Dr Devonport.

"Morning, Igor," said the doctor.

"Morning, Sir, come to check on Miss Pooky?" asked Igor politely.

"Absolutely!" replied Dr Devonport. Igor let him in just as Jack and Penelope came downstairs to see the doctor.

"Hello Wallace, nice to see you again!" said Penelope.

"You too!" smiled Dr Devonport. They headed off to the playroom. They knocked and Jack opened the door.

"Sorry to bother you lads, but Dr Devonport is here to see if Pooky is OK," explained Jack. "

Oh, that's alright, Dad, carry on!" said the twins.

The doctor walked over to Pooky. "Hello, how are you feeling today?" he asked.

"Oh, I am feeling a lot better and playing with my dolls," replied Pooky.

"Oh, that's excellent news!" Dr Devonport smiled. "I'm just going to check you over, so if you could lift up your dress then I'll be able listen to your heart," he added.

Pooky did as he asked, and the doctor placed his stethoscope on Pooky's tummy. After a few minutes the doctor said, "You're in good health, and is your arm alright?" Pooky nodded and moved it gently. "Splendid, thank you. That is all!" The doctor put all his equipment back into his case, picked it up and went out of the door to join Jack and Penelope in the living room. "Pooky is in good health and feeling a lot happier now," reported the doctor.

"That is happy news, thank you," said Penelope, and they escorted him to the door. Suddenly, as they were walking, Penelope looked down and saw some water on the floor.

"What a mess!" she said, but the doctor examined the water and took one sniff.

"That's not tap water," he cried. "It seems that your waters have broken." Jack and Penelope looked at each other and then they realised one thing.

"Oh no, the baby's coming!" cried Jack, as he knew that Penelope would soon go into labour.

"I'll take her to the bedroom and get her settled," said Dr Devonport.

"You do that, and I'll get lots of warm water and lots of towels," replied Jack.

So, while the doctor took her upstairs, breathing in and out, Jack went to the maids and said, "Penelope's gone into labour, so I'll need lots of towels and warm water right away."

Mitzi, Sophie, and Tiffany went to get everything straight away while Jack asked Igor to check on the kids and wait with them until the labour was over.

Igor did as he was asked and went to join the children in the playroom.

Meanwhile, upstairs in Jack and Penelope's bedroom, Penelope changed out of her dress into her nightdress and was lying in bed while the doctor set up his equipment, protective gloves, and apron. Then, Jack and the maids came in with towels and a bowl of warm water. Jack stood by his wife and took hold of her hand to keep her company. Poor Penelope was feeling hot and bothered and crying out in pain. She would have to push soon.

"Don't worry, Penelope, everything will be fine," said Jack.

"I really hope so," cried Penelope. "I don't know if I can breathe much longer!"

"Well, we're ready now, so I want you to push as hard as you can," Dr Devonport advised. "Are you ready Penelope?"

"Yes!" she said.

"OK. Push!" shouted the doctor. Penelope pushed as hard as she could.

"Keep pushing, keep pushing, you're doing great!" cried Jack. "I'm right here!"

After a few moments, the doctor examined the progress and cried, "Oh yes, I can see the head! Just one more push now and it will be all done!"

"Oh, I don't know if I can," wailed Penelope, as she was exhausted.

"Just one more push dear, just one more," Jack encouraged.

"OK, I'll try," Penelope cried, and gave a big almighty push.

"That's it! Almost there, almost there!" shouted Jack.

She pushed and pushed until at last, the doctor cried out, "That's it! The baby is born!"

"Wwwwhhhhhaaaaaaa!" the baby cried as the doctor cut the cord, gave it a quick wash, and wrapped it in a big warm towel.

"Well done, love!" said Jack "You did it!"

"Phew!" said Penelope, as she felt very tired.

After wrapping the baby up warmly, the doctor said, "Congratulations! You have a little baby girl!" And placed the baby into Penelope's hands.

Penelope smiled at the baby and was delighted to have another daughter. "Hello, my beautiful, sweet baby girl!" she said, and gave her a kiss on the forehead.

Jack admired her and said, "Well, now we have got two sons and two daughters!" Then he shook the doctor's hand.

"Thank you so much for your help," he smiled. "We are so grateful!"

"You're most welcome!" replied Dr Devonport. The maids looked at the baby and smiled.

"Aww, she is so cute!" said Mitzi.

"She is so lovely!" added Sophie.

Jack turned to Tiffany and asked, "Can you get Igor to bring the children upstairs please? I think it's time they saw the new-born baby."

"Of course, Sir," said Tiffany, and went off to fetch them.

Downstairs in the playroom, Pooky and Percy were still playing with the dolls and the tea sets, while Igor and the twins were playing a game of snap when Tiffany came in.

"Excuse me, I don't want to interrupt your fun, but could you all come up to your parents' room please?" asked Tiffany.

"Is there a problem?" replied Igor, looking up from his cards.

"Oh no, there's no problem, but I think they have a surprise upstairs," she said.

"Oh, I like surprises!" squawked Percy. "I wonder what it is."

"Well, let's go and see," said Pooky, and they all followed Tiffany to Jack and Penelope's bedroom. Remy saw them going upstairs and decided to go with them to see what the surprise was.

In the bedroom, Jack, Penelope, Dr Devonport, and the maids were still admiring the baby when there was a knock at the door.

"Come in," Jack called.

Tiffany opened the door just a little and said, "I've brought the children, Sir."

"Splendid, they can come in!" said Jack. So Tiffany opened the door wide and led Igor and the children in.

"Let Pooky come in front, please," said Penelope, and Pooky stepped forward.

"Children, here is your surprise!" she said and pulled back the towel so that they could the baby for the first time. Pooky, Donald and Douglas couldn't believe their eyes as they took in the sight of the wonderful little baby being cuddled in Penelope's arms.

"Oh, what a beautiful baby!" said Pooky as she stood next to the bed.

"Yes indeed!" Her mother smiled. "You and the boys have a little baby sister and that was your surprise," she added.

Pooky gazed at the baby for a moment and then she noticed that her mum's tummy wasn't big anymore and suddenly she understood.

"Oh, so that's why your tummy was big," she said, "You had a baby inside you!"

"Yes, that's right dear," Penelope said as she explained. "You see, we thought it would be nice for you and your big brothers to have a new baby to play with after everything you've been through, and things will get better now that your troubles are over."

Penelope kissed the baby on the cheek and then she said, "Would you like to be the first to hold the baby, sweetheart?"

"Yes please, Mum," Pooky said, as she happily sat on the bed next to Penelope.

Penelope handed the baby to Jack so that he could place it into Pooky's arms.

Pooky smiled at the baby and quietly spoke to it, "Hello there, you're such an adorable baby and look as pretty as a red poppy."

Jack and Penelope looked at each other and thought for a moment.

"Pretty as a red Poppy," Jack pondered, and then they both smiled. "Pooky, you're a genius!" Jack said.

Pooky felt puzzled. "What do you mean, Dad?" she asked.

"Well, you said that she is as pretty as a red poppy. You've found the perfect name for the baby," Penelope said. "And so the baby will be called Poppy."

Pooky was confused for a minute, but then she realised that she had thought of a name and quite liked the idea. "Yes, we'll call her Poppy. Poppy Beaumont!" she said, and everyone agreed.

Donald and Douglas were touched as they sat down beside Pooky and gave Poppy a warm stroke. Percy, still sitting on Pooky's shoulder, was so happy to see a new-born baby that a tear ran down his beak, and flew to perch on the bed. Igor was admiring the Beaumont family so happily that a few tears ran down his cheeks too.

Pooky gave Poppy a kiss and said, "Well I'm glad to have a wonderful family and great friends by my side and now I've got a pet parrot, as well as a good companion, a friendly witch, who once was ugly, is now a wonderful house maid and cook, and best of all, we have a new member in the family, little Poppy Beaumont."

"I quite agree, Pooky," said Donald.

"And we'll be right by her side just like we're right by your side," added Douglas.

"Well, I think we're going to have a wonderful life, now that we're back together again!" smiled Jack and hugged Penelope as she put her arm around him.

And so Pooky's troubles with Hector and Rocky and the evil wizard are over. Everyone, as well as the children in school, grew fond of her and she had lots of friends to play with. But she never forgot about the adventure she had. She is now brave, and she still has her magic powers that she uses to protect her family.

Her first adventure was over, but she knew that one day she would be able to go off on a brand-new adventure – maybe to protect her country.

The End

Pookistory

Here are some interesting historical facts about things you will read in my story:

Neanderthals lived during the Ice Age. They lived in caves to shelter from the ice and snow and became known as 'cave men'

Stone Age humans lived about two and a half million years ago. They hunted wild animals and protected themselves using primitive stone tools.

The Middle Ages describes the time in Europe between the fifth and fourteenth centuries from the fall of the Roman Empire to the start of the Renaissance.

It is also called the medieval period.

1485 – The Battle of Bosworth Field was one of the most important battles in English history. It led to the Wars of the Roses between the Lancastrians and Yorkists. King Richard III, a Yorkist, was defeated and this led to Henry Tudor, Earl of Richmond and a Lancastrian becoming the first Tudor monarch, Henry VII. He reigned until 1509.

1485–1603 – The Tudors reigned

1596 – Sir John Harrington invented the first flushing toilet for Queen Elizabeth 1. He was a courtier and her godson

1603–1714 – The Stuarts reigned

1816 – The first stethoscope was invented by Rene Laennec. Here is what it looked like and a more modern version.

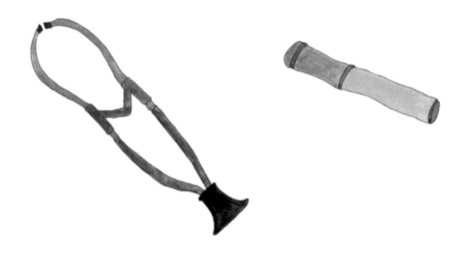

1837–1901 Queen Victoria reigned.

1830s and 1840s – Drawers started to be worn by women.

Tights had been worn since 1803.

1858 – The Great Stink of London was created by the hot summer of 1858, when raw sewage in the River Thames began to decompose, releasing nasty fumes into the air which affected 'everyone' who went near the river, including the Members of Parliament. This, together with the frequent outbreaks of cholera, led to work on sewers and street improvements. By 1866 most of London was connected to a sewer network devised by chief engineer, Joseph Bazalgette. Work was still being done until the 1890s.

1860s – Gas lights were used for lighting in houses. Thomas Edison patented the first electric light in 1878.

1876 – Alexander Graham Bell patented the first telephone (after the inventions by Antonio Meucci in 1849 and Charles Bourseul in 1854). From 1879 telephones started to be used in wealthy private houses.

1880s – Bicycles became popular as an alternative to the penny farthing as they were considered safer.

1885 – Dr Georges Gilles de la Tourette first described the condition where people make involuntary movements and sounds called 'tics'.

1888 – The connection between chicken pox virus and the shingles virus was first noted.

William Heberden had shown that chicken pox was different to smallpox in 1867.

Night Soil Men: Before sewers were invented there were men who did the mucking out of cess pools and privies at night and transported the human waste away from urban areas. They were called the 'night soil' men or the 'gong farmers'. Being a night soil man wasn't exactly a dream job, but it paid well, and many did it as a part-time job.

The men usually worked in teams of four: one acted as a hole man, the other a rope man, and two were tub men. The hole man was the one who crawled into the cess pool to scoop up the waste into a bucket. The rope man then hauled the bucket up and passed it to the tub men, who took the buckets to a cart to be carried away.

Irritable Bowel Syndrome is a term that started to be used in the 1950s to describe a group of symptoms such as stomach ache, gas and bloating, and diarrhoea. This is what Pooky suffered from.

Fathers being present at the birth was not common in Victorian times but there were some exceptions in wealthy households like the Beaumont family. Prince Albert was present when Queen Victoria gave birth to some of their children.